B

UN
GROUND

ISABELLE MARINOV

Clock Tower Publishing, an imprint of
Sweet Cherry Publishing Limited
Unit 36, Vulcan House,
Vulcan Road,
Leicester, LE5 3EF
United Kingdom

Children's Publisher of the Year 2022

First published in the UK in 2023
2023 edition

2 4 6 8 10 9 7 5 3 1

ISBN: 978-1-78226-9755

Cover design by Sophie Jones
Cover illustrations by Paula Zorite
Internal illustrations by Arthur Kearns, Jessica Walters, Jess Brown,
Amy Booth, Matt Ellero and Sophie Jones

www.clocktowerpublishing.com

Printed and bound in Turkey

For Eli and Jonah

CONTENTS

1km

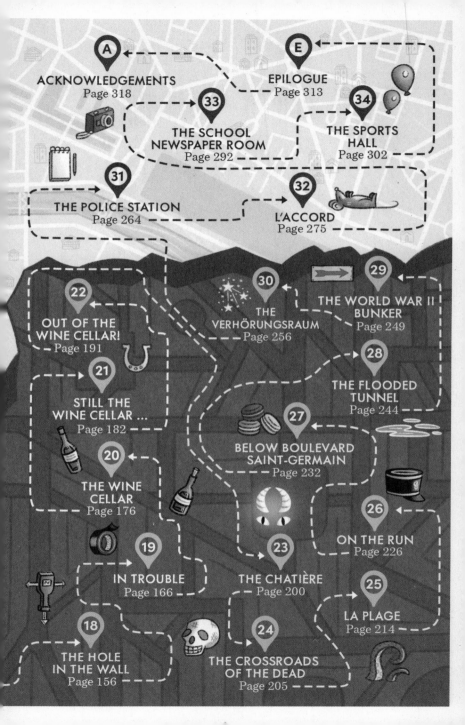

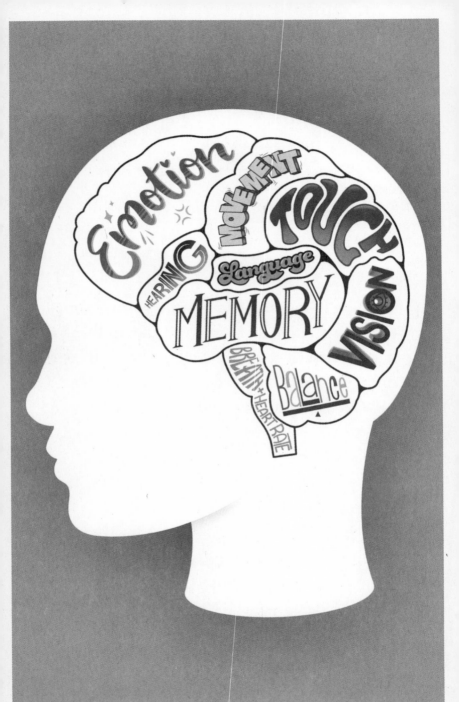

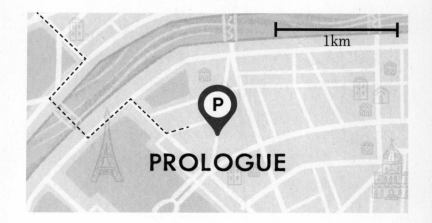

PROLOGUE

Did you know that the brain can be mapped, just like a country or a city? I like to think of it as the main circuit board of the body, with different parts in charge of different tasks.

My brain probably looks just like anyone else's. Mathilde, my therapist, says that if you looked at my brain, you couldn't tell that my circuitry has trouble transmitting the different data it receives. There's no sign that says my senses are extra sensitive to stimulation. That I can smell a melon being cut two rooms away, or that the sun is too bright for me even on cloudy days. As for controlling the volume of my voice when

I'm excited – impossible! It's like I need to speak louder to hear myself over my thoughts because my brain is so busy processing all the information.

My brain can do some really cool stuff. I have a photographic memory. I can take detailed mental pictures of things I see, even if it's just briefly, and store them for later. My mental photo album is HUGE. Only you can't tell because the brain doesn't reveal its workings the way other organs in the body do. The heart pumps blood. Kidneys filter waste. It's pretty obvious what they do just by looking at them. But the brain is, despite all modern medical knowledge, still a mystery. Which is why the idea of a 'typical' one is strange to me, or that mine is somehow 'divergent'. I only know what's typical for me. *Hugo*.

And typically, I like to begin my stories with a map …

① THE SWIMMING POOL

Here's a map we're all familiar with: the map of the world.

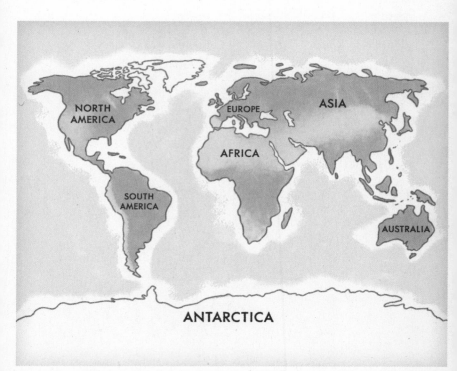

But two hundred million years ago, the world looked very different. That's because all the continents – Asia, Africa, North America, South America, Antarctica, Europe and Australia – were glued together in one huge *super*continent called Pangea.

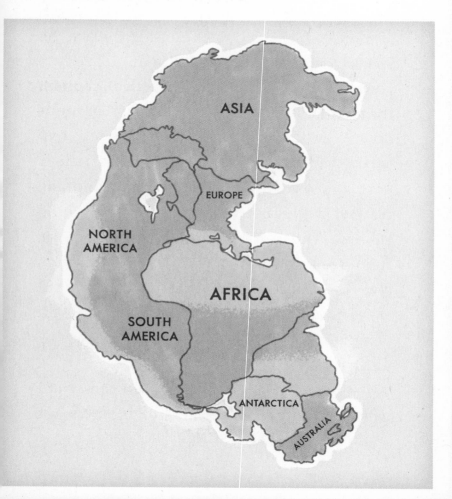

Then the continents drifted apart.

That's what happened to me and my friends, Alex and Julie. Slowly they just drifted away from me. Now Julie reminds me of Australia. She loves the water (minus the sharks), and three weeks ago she broke the record in the fifty-metre butterfly. Alex is like North America: loud and self-confident, like he speaks and lives in capital letters.

Me, I feel more like Antarctica: remote, isolated and with a permanent risk of meltdown. Right now, on our weekly school trip to the indoor swimming pool, that risk is particularly high. It's too loud. The swimming teacher's whistle, the voices – everything echoes. And don't get me started on the fluorescent lights. All I want is to cover my ears and shield my eyes and hide in a corner until we're done. My brain is so busy dealing with just the *smell* that I have a hard time focussing on anything else.

I'm near the shallow end of the pool, right where only my toes touch the bottom. It's just enough to reassure me that I can run away if I want to. Everyone else is further out, swimming.

Most of us have been playing water polo for the past fifteen minutes and I haven't had the ball once. That's fine with me and the new swimming teacher, who only has eyes for stars like Julie. Right now she's gliding along one of the lanes like a dolphin – one with straight black hair and brown freckles.

Four years ago, when she was eight, Julie started to develop a curved spine. It's called 'Scheuermann's Disease', but a couple of girls in our class made fun of her and called her a hunchback. It made Julie very sad, so I told her facts about maps that made her smile. That's how we became friends. But then Julie's doctor told her parents that she should take up swimming to help straighten her back. Not only did her back straighten, but she became really good at swimming. I mean *really* good.

Since then, things have changed between us. She doesn't seem to be interested in hearing about maps, and she never invites me over anymore.

'Hey, Spy!' A voice booms. 'Close your mouth, you'll swallow a fly!'

My name is Hugo but everyone calls me Spy because I often wear sunglasses, even when it's not sunny. Apparently I look like I'm wearing a really bad disguise, but it's because my eyes are super sensitive to light.

A few people laugh at what Alex has said, but the echo makes it sound like more.

Alex and I used to be friends too. We would group our toy cars by model and colour during playdates. Well, *I* would. Alex would share his encyclopedic knowledge of all things automobile with me. Like the fact that it would take less than six months to get to the moon by car travelling at a hundred kilometres per hour. And if you parked all the cars in the world bonnet to boot, the line would stretch from Sydney to London, then back to Sydney, then back to London, then Sydney again. But that was calculated a few years ago, so who knows how far the line stretches now? Not that it matters. These days Alex just makes fun of me. Seventy-four days ago he emptied a carton of milk over my head. I still don't know why.

Alex throws the water polo ball to me. It hits my nose and splashes out of play. With the teacher distracted, the other players' eyes turn to me.

'You're supposed to catch the ball,' someone says.

I know that. My brain just has trouble telling my arms what to do sometimes.

'He's too busy watching Julie,' Alex snorts.

'You wanna join her, Spy? Show her your moves?' A new voice joins in, and then another.

'I bet he does a killer butterfly, don't you, Spy?'

'Go on, Spy! Time for a new school record!'

Suddenly there's a chorus of voices, rising in a strangely hypnotic chant that bounces off every surface, crowding me from all sides: 'Go, Spy, go!'

The teacher's whistle blows. 'Back to the game!' he shouts.

My ears ring from the noise. My nose stings from the ball. The fluorescent tubes on the ceiling turn into stage lights, getting brighter by the second. I can feel myself losing control. I need to distract my brain.

I glance at Julie. She's just climbed out of the pool, looking strong and determined in her dark blue swimming costume. Someone hands her a towel. She glances my way but doesn't seem to see me. I want her to listen to my stories again. I want things to be like they used to be.

'Go, Spy, go!'

Maybe I just need to remind her that I exist?

'Go, Spy, go!'

At the very least I can escape the noise.

I take a deep breath and plunge into the water, throwing my arms forward and kicking my feet. The result is a belly flop and a nose full of chlorine. It's unlikely to impress Julie, but the voices are finally muted, the lights are dulled. I stop swimming for a moment and let myself float just under the surface. Bubbles escape my nose, letting me sink a little deeper. And the deeper I go the quieter the world becomes. The pressure of the water is like a tight hug, a liquid blanket enveloping me. It feels so good.

I can hold my breath for a very long time. I used to practise in the bathtub while Mum or my sister Zoé timed me. My personal record is one minute and three seconds.

I close my eyes and imagine I'm diving down to red coral reefs, swimming alongside colourful striped fish and anemones swaying in the current. I kick my way to the bottom of the pool and try to stay there without letting more oxygen out of my lungs, which is hard. Archimedes' Law means that any object less dense than the surrounding water will naturally float back to the surface, like my body is trying to do now. I smile at the memory of Zoé congratulating me on being less 'dense' than water. That was a good joke.

Then something grabs me. Before I know what's happening, my head is cresting the surface of the pool. Next my whole body is hauled out of the water and I feel cold, as if someone has pulled my cosy duvet off me.

The swimming teacher lays me on the floor. I stiffen, thinking about all the bare, verruca-infested feet that have walked over these tiles.

'Put him on his side!' someone shouts. 'Check his lungs for water!'

'Is he still breathing?'

'His eyes are open!'

I try to tell them that I wasn't about to drown and that I didn't need saving, but I'm too dazed by the return of the fluorescent lights and echoes. While everyone confirms the obvious, I squint at the other end of the pool where Julie has long since disappeared.

Just this once, I'm glad she didn't notice me.

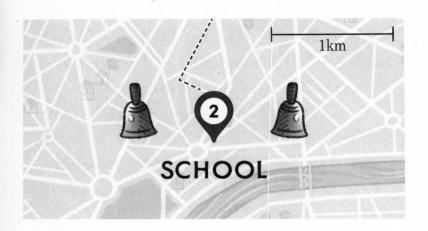

Julie is always busy these days. Whether she's on her way to the pool for swimming practice or to the school library for homework, it's like her life no longer has time for activities with no obvious goal – such as the exchange of interesting map facts.

That's why I decided to write to her.

The letter will take just over a minute to read. I timed myself and it took me fifty-eight seconds and twenty-one milliseconds, but I wrote it, so I would add extra seconds for someone who's unfamiliar with its content. And everyone has a minute to spare. Even Julie.

Dear Julie,

A year and 187 days ago we were in P.E. together. Remember? It was a Monday and it was raining. You wore a blue T-shirt with white shorts.

Mademoiselle Dutronc asked us to do a backbend. Most of the girls were really good at it, especially Sophie and Pénélope. They dropped back without any help, their arms pressing into the ground like pillars, their spines curved in a perfect arch. I was less flexible, like most of the boys. Mademoiselle Dutronc gave me a large plastic ball to lay my back on and bend over backwards. In the end, even I managed to do it, although my arch was more like a flattened crescent.

You were the only one who couldn't bend backwards, not even on the ball. Mademoiselle Dutronc told you to open your chest and your shoulders, and you said you couldn't. She said that wasn't possible — that everybody could. You told Mademoiselle Dutronc that you had back problems and she said you were too young to have back problems. And then Sophie and Pénélope started giggling and calling you Quasimodo from *The Hunchback of Notre Dame*. Your face turned red from anger or embarrassment, or maybe from both. All I know is that I made you laugh when I told you later, during breaktime, that if you combine South America with Africa, you get the head of an Allosaurus. Lake Victoria becomes the dinosaur's eye, and the Argentinian coast becomes its lower jaw.

Do you remember this?

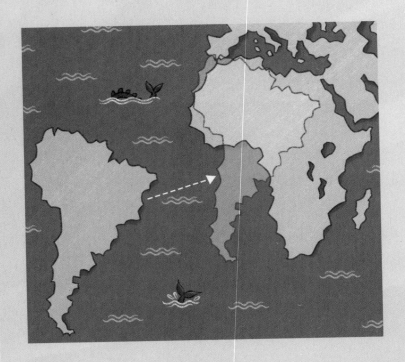

After that, I told you a new map fact every time you looked sad. But then you took up swimming and you became really good at it. You hung out with the kids in your swimming team, with the large shoulders and small waists that make their bodies look like the letter V.

Nobody called you a hunchback anymore.

Since then, you've drifted away from me, but I haven't given up hope that you might make a U-turn and that we will drift back together again: you and me, and even Alex.

I hope you enjoy the picture of the Allosaurus.

Your friend,

Hugo

I wrote the letter at breaktime, with my hair still damp from the swimming pool. I printed it out at lunch. By fifth period I'd managed to slip it into Julie's rucksack. It's the end of the day now and I don't think she's found it yet. But she will. And she'll love it. Who doesn't love letters?

Even if it doesn't have cool stamps on it like the postcards Dad sends when he's away. Even if it's not handwritten. A letter means that the message inside it is important. I want Julie to know that when she reads mine. Maybe she'll even keep it like I do the postcards from Dad …

The school bell rings. The shrill, high-pitched sound reverberates through my body – even though I put my noise-cancelling headphones on ahead of time. At the classroom door I just about manage to take the flyer my form tutor is handing out, then I'm swept along with a tide of people pushing and shoving, screaming and laughing. I would rather wait until everyone has left, but I'm too afraid I'll miss the bus.

I notice that these flyers have popped up everywhere: in the locker area, along the corridors and all the way to the school entrance. I look down at the one in my hand.

FANCY DRESS PARTY

Date: June 12th, 5 p.m.
Theme: **SUPERHEROES**

A figure walks beside me and I move my headphones down around my neck.

'Are you going?' Enzo asks as we head towards the school bus.

Enzo is one of Alex's followers. Alex's followers always laugh at his jokes. They bring him food in the canteen. Sometimes they even do his homework for him. In exchange, they get his protection from outside attacks. If you're part of Alex's group, nobody dares to mess with you. Alex considers an attack against any of his followers an attack against him. A bit like NATO, I guess. Or a Mafia boss. It makes sense for Enzo to be part of that group. He's twelve, like me, but he looks like he only just turned seven.

'No,' I say. 'I don't like parties.' Which is not entirely true. I might like them if I knew how to talk to other kids so that they'd let me hang out with them. Mathilde says I need to work on my 'communication skills'.

Then, because Mathilde says it's good to ask questions: 'Are you going?' I ask. 'Who will you go as?'

'Iron Man,' Enzo says. 'My mum's making my costume using real LED lights.'

'I'm not sure Iron Man's your best choice.'

'Why not? He's the strongest.'

'Exactly,' I say. 'You're really small for your age. And then there's your voice. You have a girl's voice.'

Enzo gives me a blank stare.

'You won't make a believable Iron Man, is what I'm saying. You're more like Spider-Man,' I suggest. 'He's skinny. And I'm sure your mum can change the costume. Spider-Man's suit is red and blue, and Iron Man's is red and gold.

She can just swap the gold for blue and you'll be good to go. Except for your voice, but I guess you can't change that.'

'Wow.' Enzo is shaking his head. 'That was mean ...'

It's my turn to look blank.

'I'm not being mean. I think Spider-Man's cool too.' I hold up three fingers the way Spider-Man does when he's about to fire his webbing. My hand is shaking a little. I'm panicking. I don't like this.

'No wonder no one wants to hang out with you.'

Enzo's words hit me like the water polo ball, this time straight to the stomach.

'I'm sorry,' I tell him. 'But it's the truth. I'm not good at lying.'

'Just being mean,' Enzo says. And he walks off alone even though we're both heading to the same place.

Sometimes, even when I try to be friendly, it comes out wrong. I'm like a magnet that's poled the wrong way: repelling instead of attracting.

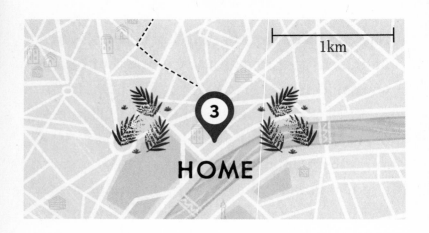

3

HOME

'Hey, Hugo. What's up?' Zoé asks, inspecting her hair in the hallway mirror.

When I said I have no friends, that wasn't entirely true. Zoé is my friend, but she's also my sister so I'm not sure if she counts. Either way, for the longest time, I never had to make any effort to win her over. Zoé always liked it when I told her things. She always listened to me. And she never expected me to ask her questions to show that I was interested in how she felt and what she thought. I never had to apply all the complicated conversation rules that Mathilde tries to teach me.

But lately things have changed with Zoé

too. Ever since she turned fourteen (145 days ago), she no longer listens to me. Not in the way she used to. She's too busy looking in mirrors. That includes real mirrors, but also shop windows, Mum's silver teapot, windows at night, and probably the gold-coated visor of a space helmet if she ever met an astronaut. She hasn't, but you get my point. All she needs is a reflective surface.

'Omigosh, look at that frizz,' Zoé sighs, trying to flatten her blonde fringe with her fingers. 'My hair looks like sauerkraut.'

Her friend Lisa peeks over her shoulder. 'I think it's cute,' she says.

'I want to get it straightened.'

'Your hair comes out curly because your hair follicle is oval instead of round,' I say. 'Even if you straighten it, it'll just grow back curly.'

Zoé rolls her eyes and sighs. That's something she never did before, either.

'Hugo,' she says, 'thanks for your scientific input, but this is girl stuff. You don't understand.'

Clearly.

'How was school?' Zoé asks, turning her attention back to her reflection. 'Heard you almost drowned.'

'Where did you hear that?'

'The school called Mum. Don't be surprised if she tries to film you holding your breath at some point just to prove how long you can do it for. I don't think they believed her.'

'It doesn't matter,' I say, rubbing against the wall.

Rubbing against a wall feels like taking a hot bath, or spinning a drinks coaster on its edge until it falls. It calms me down when I need it – which is whenever I come home from school. School is stressful and tiring.

'Don't do that,' Zoé whispers, pointing at the faded palm leaf that marks my favourite spot on the wall. 'That wallpaper was super expensive.'

'What's he doing?' Lisa asks.

'I told you before, Hugo's brain is wired a bit differently,' Zoé explains, when I don't answer myself. 'Noises, smells and lights can

28

overwhelm him, and that can be pretty stressful. Rubbing calms him down. It's called stimming – look it up.'

At least some things with Zoé haven't changed. If she wasn't my sister, I could hire her as my spokesperson. She always wants people to understand me better, but doesn't think it's my job to teach them if I don't want to.

I stop rubbing and take my water bottle out of my rucksack to give to Mum, catching the flyer before it flutters to the floor. Suddenly Mum is standing next to me, wearing the apron I made her at school for Mother's Day. The smell of lemon and garlic clings to it.

'Come here, you.' Mum holds her arms out and pulls me in for a tight hug. As she stands back, the flyer uncrumples between us. 'What's this?' she says, plucking it from my hand. 'A superhero party? That's so perfect for you! My little Aquaman.'

Mum always says that I'm a superhero. And while I don't wear a cape or have a secret identity, I can't deny that I share some features.

'Cover your ears, Hugo!' Mum says as I follow her into the kitchen. 'I need to use the mixer.'

Like Superman, I have super hearing. My ears pick up everything around me even at a distance, from the buzzing of bees to the drilling of street compressors. High-pitched, shrill noises are the worst. Like those of kitchen utensils. Or really loud noises like the trailers before a film. The last time I went to the cinema without my ear defenders, I ran out before the film even started.

'We need to leave in an hour for therapy,' Mum says.

I see Mathilde, my therapist, every second Friday. Mum usually takes me as Dad is away most of the time. His job is to travel the world and tell everyone how great French champagne is. I don't really see the point because everyone knows that already.

I hear Zoé and Lisa's giggles coming from the hallway and feel a glimmer of jealousy.

'Mum?' I blurt out, as she puts on her gloves

and takes a tray from the oven. 'How do I make friends?'

Mum stops for a moment and gives me a surprised look. She quickly puts down the hot tray. The smell of garlic bread fills my nose.

'What about Alex and Julie?' she says. 'Aren't they your friends anymore?'

'I don't think so.'

'Why is that?'

'I don't know. Just answer my question: how do I make friends?'

'I guess by being yourself.'

I'm myself all the time. Who else would I be?

'That way,' she continues, 'you'll find kids with the same interests as you.'

Maybe that's the problem. I mean, what are the chances I'll find someone who shares my fascination with the London tube map?

I don't know. I love Mum, but I think I need professional advice.

MATHILDE'S OFFICE

'So because of what happened with Enzo today, you want to talk about friendship?' Mathilde asks from behind her large white desk. She rests her elbows on the table and cups her chin. All I can focus on is the ring on her right hand. The dark green stone covers half her finger. Lighter green waves swirl across the stone like milk in Mum's coffee. Whenever I see something beautiful and intriguing like Mathilde's ring, the world around me stops for a moment to let me analyse it.

'Hugo? Are you listening?'

'Yes,' I reply. 'I used to have friends, but they don't seem to be interested in me anymore.'

'Why is that?' Mathilde leans back in her chair. She smells nice today, like citrus, echoing the bright new colours on the walls now that the paint smell has finally faded.

'I don't know.'

'Well, you know, Hugo, people change. Our interests change. We grow apart. That's true for everyone. Especially now, at the age of twelve. Have you tried to make new friends? Is that what you were doing with Enzo?'

I shrug. I don't want new friends. I hate change. I want to be friends with Alex and Julie again. I want to go back to when people cared more about what was fun than what looked cool. Passing a balloon with Alex and trying to hit it near his Fart Ninja's motion sensor so that it played one of nine different fart sounds? *That* was fun. Trying to make bao buns that were 'fluffy like a cloud' with Julie (and her mum)? Well, that was fun *and* frustrating, because mine always came out of the bamboo steamer rubbery. But Julie always let me have hers.

'Why do you think Enzo was mad at you?'

Mathilde interrupts my thoughts.

'I have no idea. Your ring is huge.'

Mathilde sighs. She knows me well enough to understand that I don't like to talk about my failures. She's been my occupational therapist for eight years.

'Was it because you offended him?' she asks.

'He wouldn't be a convincing Iron Man!' I say. It's the truth. Why am I not allowed to say it?

'I know it can be tricky, Hugo, but to make friends you need to understand what the other person is feeling. Enzo was proud of his Iron Man costume, and you didn't notice that. That's why he was upset and walked away.'

'But he would be a *perfect* Spider-Man.' I fold my arms. 'Having a conversation is so complicated. I think I might need the social story cards again.'

A couple of years ago, Mathilde lent me a set of cards designed to teach social skills. Since these skills didn't develop naturally for me, Mathilde encouraged me to learn them like a new language.

Mathilde looks surprised.

'You don't need them anymore, Hugo. You're doing great.'

'Please?'

After a moment, Mathilde gets up. She runs her finger – the one with the giant green ring on it – along book spines with titles like *Autism Spectrum Disorder* and *Communication Skills Made Easy*. 'Ah! Here they are.' She hands me a shallow box. I remove a few laminated cards and read their titles: 'Starting a conversation'. 'Giving compliments'. 'Recognising emotions in others'. 'Telling jokes'.

I stuff the box of cards into my rucksack. It will be a refresher course for me. I'm pretty good at learning languages. I still remember some Mandarin words from Julie. Plus I even invented my own language called Kielppo, with grammar rules and everything. Zoé and I are the only two people in the entire world who speak Kielppo – if she still remembers it.

'Now, let's ask your mum to come in,' Mathilde says finally.

Mathilde and I always have ten minutes of 'private time' before Mum joins our sessions. I'm grateful for that because it gives me a chance to discuss secret stuff with her. Mathilde says that she's not allowed to tell Mum anything about what we discuss during this time. It's called the 'therapist-patient privilege'. Basically, Mathilde could go to prison if she breaks it.

'Hugo,' Mathilde says, 'why don't you relax in the hammock while I chat with your mum?'

Mathilde's office looks more like a play centre. It has ball pits, giant mattresses and colourful pillows – even a hammock suspended from the ceiling. While Mum takes my place in front of the big desk, I look out the window and swing back and forth, overhearing her mention 'pool' and 'rubbing'.

To someone from the outside, my therapy sessions probably look like playtime. I swing in the hammock, swim in the ball pit and, at Mathilde's urging, jump over mattresses and into pillows. What's really happening is that she's trying to rewire my brain. Certain parts of it, anyway. Because there's a lot I like about my brain that I wouldn't want to change. Like being able to remember literally everything without effort. Or thinking in pictures, like my brain is doing a Google image search for me. For a long time, I thought that everyone's brain worked like that. But apparently they don't, which is a shame.

Then there are other things about my brain that I just accept as part of me. Like the fact that I have trouble visualising where my body is in space. Most people know their body limits. They don't have to consciously think about it. But when I'm really tired, I can't tell where my body starts and where it ends. That's why I like to feel pressure on my body to remind me.

'Your mum is worried about you, Hugo,' Mathilde begins.

'Mum isn't worried about me,' I say, swinging back and forth in the hammock. 'She's worried about her wallpaper.'

'Hugo!' Mum exclaims. Mathilde chuckles. Did I just make a joke? I didn't mean to.

'Your mum loves you very much, Hugo.'

'Of course I do! Much more than the wallpaper.'

'I think we should try a weighted vest again,' Mathilde continues, playing with her colourful beaded necklace. Mathilde likes to wear chunky jewellery, which is weird because she's so small. I worry that one day she'll collapse under the weight of it all.

'The vest puts soft pressure on the wearer's shoulders,' Mathilde explains, 'like a kind of soothing sensory hug. It has a tremendously calming effect. What do you think, Hugo? Would you like to give it another go?'

'Maybe.'

One thing I really like about Mathilde is that she always asks for my opinion. She treats me like a grown-up. It works well when we're alone; less well when Mum is with us.

'It sounds wonderful!' Mum enthuses, taking over the conversation. 'Of course, we'll try it. Right, Hugo?'

Mathilde first suggested the vest when I

was six years old, and back then I didn't like it. It made me feel like I couldn't breathe. But that was a long time ago. I didn't even like broccoli back then. Now it's my favourite vegetable.

Mathilde opens the cupboard behind her desk and takes out a blue sleeveless vest. 'It comes filled with sand,' she explains, stroking it like a pet. 'You can adjust the weight by taking out or adding sand pouches.'

'And it looks so stylish!' Mum accepts the vest and holds it at arm's length to admire it. 'Nobody would ever guess it's a therapeutic vest.'

I frown. The vest may be useful for calming me down. It may keep me warm. Its weight could also probably keep me safely glued to the moon's surface, or to any other satellite object or planet with similarly low gravity. But 'stylish'?

I slide out of the hammock and put it on. It's bulky. The thick sand pouches make me look like I've been inflated. I don't know what people will think when they see me wearing this, but I doubt 'Oh, I wish I had a vest like Hugo's!' will be it.

There's no price tag. Dad always says that's how you know something's expensive. Maybe even more expensive than Darth Vader's Castle on Planet Mustafar, the *Star Wars* Lego set Mum refused to buy me last week because she wasn't ready to spend so much money on 'a couple of plastic bricks and three ugly figurines'.

I close the vest's three front straps. A sense of calmness instantly washes over me. For the past ten minutes, a part of me has been in the garden with the birds. Another part has been wondering whether the pale orange and green of the office walls goes well together or not. And still another part has been trying to decide whether Mathilde's perfume smells more of lemons or limes. Somehow, wearing the vest brings the scattered parts of me back together again, like pieces of a puzzle assembled inside the box, or spilt liquid poured back into a glass.

'So, what do you think, Hugo?' Mathilde asks encouragingly.

I think it's hideous. I think I won't wear it. I think it'll get Alex and Julie's attention in completely the wrong way if I do. But ...

'It feels good,' I admit. 'Like taking a hot bath. Or rubbing against the wall.'

'Well, you won't have to do that anymore!' Mum cheers. 'Not with that nifty vest.'

That's another word that doesn't apply to this vest: 'nifty'. But Mum is smiling and Mathilde is giving me two thumbs up, so I guess either way it's mine.

I'd just rather have Darth Vader's Castle on Planet Mustafar.

THE JARDIN DES PLANTES

Today, Monsieur Portmann, our science teacher, has taken us to the *Jardin des Plantes*, the botanical garden in the *5th arrondissement*. We took the Métro line 11 and then changed at *Châtelet* for line 7. It's the fastest route, despite the fact that *Châtelet* is the busiest station on the Paris Métro.

Julie is wearing her yellow dress, the one that makes her look like a buttercup. She hasn't said anything about the letter and it's Monday now. Maybe she hasn't found it yet. I will give her until tomorrow.

🌿 THE JARDIN DES PLANTES 🌿

We enter the greenhouses at the *Jardin des Plantes*. My sunglasses instantly fog up. Monsieur Portmann takes a patterned handkerchief out of his pocket and hands it to me. The greenhouses – when I can see again – look like cathedrals made of glass and metal. Monsieur Portmann informs us that they're fifteen metres high.

LE JARDIN DES PLANTES

E Entrée
X Restaurant
+ Premiers Secours
WC Toilettes
i Informations
⛺ Aire de pique-nique

GALERIE DE GÉOLOGIE ET DE MINÉRALOGIE

LABYRINTHE

SERRE DE L'HISTOIRE DES PLANTES

SERRE DES DÉSERTS ET MILIEUX ARIDES

SERRE DES FORÊTS TROPICALES HUMIDES

GALERIE DE BOTANIQUE

JARDIN ALPIN

It's warm and damp inside. The air smells green. Like when you chew fresh spearmint gum and for the first ten seconds the taste explodes in your mouth until you can't think of anything but the amazing greenness of it.

Monsieur Portmann tells us about the ferns and the orchids, and all the other tropical plants and trees in the greenhouses. My eyes wander to the dome above our heads. There are so many individual panes of glass.

Monsieur Portmann moves on to telling us all about the *laboratoire des catacombes*. Apparently, in the 19th century, scientists at the *Jardin des Plantes* set up an underground lab to study how insects and fish would develop without natural light. I stop counting to listen more closely. I know about the old ossuaries below Paris where human bones were stored after the cemeteries started overflowing in the 18th century. But is there more down there?

'The catacombs are just a tiny part of the underground,' Monsieur Portmann explains. 'Below Paris there's a labyrinth of tunnels and caverns more than 250 kilometres long. Most of it is made of old quarries, where they dug out the limestone to build the city. There's a bunker, too, from World War II – but that's a story for another time. Let's focus on the lab for today.'

Who can focus on insects and fish after that? There's a dark, flipped side of our city below us! The negative image of Paris, right beneath our feet! I scan the group for someone to share my excitement with. Julie is taking a selfie with kids from the swimming team, a banana tree in the background. Alex is sneaking a wet leaf down Enzo's jumper. Nobody seems to care.

'How did they get down there?' I ask in a rush. 'How was the *Jardin des Plantes* connected to the underground? Did they have to enter through the catacombs?'

'No, they used an old well to get down there,' Monsieur Portmann replies. 'Armand Viré, the director of the *Jardin des Plantes* in the late 19th century, was fascinated by caves. He studied them and their lifeforms, and was curious to know how creatures that live on the surface would fare without sunlight. To find out, he collected fish and insects and brought them to his underground lab. What do you think happened to them down there? Any ideas?' He looks around, clearly trying to infuse some energy into the group.

Alex yawns. 'They died?'

'No. Well, maybe some did ...'

'They adapted?' I suggest. 'To suit their new environment?'

'Excellent, Hugo!' Monsieur Portmann says triumphantly. '*Adaptation*. That's what evolution is all about, right? Remember Darwin?'

'Know-it-all,' Alex mutters.

I think he means me. But I wouldn't say I know *all* about adaptation. I just know a lot. After all, I adapt every day to a world that isn't made for kids like me.

Monsieur Portmann is still speaking. 'Underground, the fish lost their natural colouring due to the darkness. The insects' sense of sight became weaker and their mechanoreceptors became larger – meaning stronger.'

'What are mechanoreceptors?' I like the sound of that word.

'They're like sensors. They allow insects to feel the space around them and their position within it – a way of seeing without seeing, if you will. Very useful in the dark!'

'Do humans have mechanoreceptors?'

'Yes, Hugo. Our skin has lots of them.'

If that's the case, then mine are definitely out of sync. Would they be better underground? Like the insects'?

Before I can ask, Monsieur Portmann waves us forward. 'Come on!' he says. 'Let's move on to the ferns!'

Reluctantly, the class and I follow.

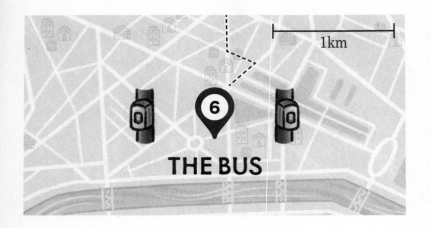

THE BUS

We return to school for afternoon lessons, but by then my concentration is waning. Someone is mowing grass outside. The orchestra is rehearsing in the sports hall. The classroom still smells of bleach after last week's Salmonella outbreak in the canteen prompted school-wide disinfection. Sunlight is peaking through the blinds, prickling my eyes like a thousand tiny needles. I have to put my sunglasses on.

A meltdown is a bit like a volcano erupting. Before it spits lava, the mountain sends out warning signs, shaking the earth and puffing steam. My quickening heartbeat is like the steam, but my eruption is still a way off.

I think of the vest in my school bag as I look around me. Everyone is immersed in their biology books, drawing the human cell for our latest project. The nucleus in red, the mitochondria in blue. Alex and Julie have been paired together. I'm on my own since the class is an odd number.

Would now be a good time?

Monsieur Portmann sees me looking around and comes over. 'Are you OK, Hugo?' he asks quietly. 'Do you need to go next door?'

The room next to our classroom is my safe space, where I can rest when I'm exhausted or when the world around me is getting too intense.

I shake my head and reach under my desk, not wanting to attract more attention than necessary by saying what I'm doing. Seeing me retrieve my rucksack, however, Monsieur Portmann gives me an encouraging nod and walks away.

Mum must have already told him about the vest, which confirms my suspicion that her claiming 'nobody would ever guess it's a therapeutic vest' was a lie. Why else would he need to be informed? Mum didn't call him after she bought me a new winter coat.

The moment I put on the vest, the muscles in my body relax. No more earthquakes. No more steam. The outside pressure balances the inside pressure like an equalizer. My heart stops pounding. My breathing slows.

This thing really works!

I immediately add Zoé's denim shirt over the top. I came up with this idea last night. Since Zoé is way taller than me, the shirt functions as a sort of tent, like the ones police erect around evidence at a crime scene.

Because I don't want any witnesses.

I keep the vest on for the rest of school, but the bus ride home is so hot that I take off Zoé's shirt. Nobody seems to notice. Maybe Mum was right and the vest doesn't look so bad after all. And it definitely works. I'm not bothered by the chatter around me, or by the music playing at the back of the bus through Enzo's phone. It's like wearing a raincoat in the rain. Nothing gets past the outer layer before washing to the ground.

For some reason the back of the bus is reserved for rich kids, like Julie, and cool kids, like Alex. What is it about that uncomfortable bench seat and its unspecified capacity that makes it so popular? I have no idea. But it's an unwritten rule. The funny thing is, the rule doesn't apply to other means of transportation. Take planes, for instance. Rich people travel in first class, which is usually closest to the cockpit at the front. Same for trains. Sitting in the last carriage there doesn't make you look cool. It only makes you walk further to reach the ticket barrier once you arrive.

'Hey, Sailor!' Alex shouts suddenly. 'What's with the life jacket? Afraid the bus will sink?'

Laughter penetrates the vest.

'Oh no, wait! I know! He wears it so he won't drown when he's practising the butterfly!'

As the back of the bus explodes with more laughter, I turn to see Alex flailing his arms, pretending to drown.

'I wasn't drowning, I was diving,' I say.

'Yeah, right.' Alex splutters and appears to go under again.

Anger bubbles inside me. I think about taking a sand pouch from the vest and throwing it in his face when he comes back up for 'air'. But Mathilde has taught me a trick to calm myself in situations like these. She says this trick works for everyone, including herself. All you do is focus on something you find more interesting than your anger. For me, that includes the technical features of the vest.

'This vest wouldn't stop me drowning,' I inform Alex. 'It's actually the opposite. The pouches are filled with sand, which makes it very heavy – heavier than water. That's why, if I wore it swimming, it would pull me down – unlike a life jacket filled with air. Air weighs less than the water it displaces. That's why it floats. It's called buoyancy.'

I glance at Julie to see if she's impressed by my knowledge of physics. She's sitting by the window with her eyes closed and her head tipped against the glass. Her ears are clamped between the enormous white cups of her headphones. My own are in my bag. Maybe I should put them on so I can block out the noise too.

'Ladies and gentlemen, there is a life vest under your seat!' Alex pinches his nose, imitating a flight attendant's voice through a plane tannoy. 'In the unlikely event of a water landing, this vest will help you drown even quicker 'cause some moron filled it with sand!'

The laughter makes the vest seem flimsy. It keeps none of it out. I decide it's too late for headphones. The laughter is inside me now, vibrating. And I've run out of calming strategies.

'If you feel your anger rising, just walk away,' Mathilde always says. I press the red STOP button closest to me and open the maps app on my phone. If I get out here, I'll have to walk 1.2 kilometres.

'So long, Sailor!' Alex shouts as the bus pulls over. 'Hey, what happened to your shirt? Loved the pretty rose!' I don't turn around. Zoé warned me that people might notice the embroidery on the back of her shirt.

I jump off the bus and start walking. At the next intersection, I take off the vest and stuff it into a bin.

Mum greets me in the hallway when I get home. 'You're late! How did it go with the vest? Was it helpful?'

I brush past her, throwing my schoolbag on the floor. Why did she and Mathilde insist on that stupid vest? I should have trusted my instincts. Even to me, that thing looked weird.

Mum takes me by my shoulders.

'Did the other kids make fun of you?'

I look away. 'Where's Zoé?' I ask.

'She's spending the night at Lisa's.'

I feel a pulling sensation in my gut. A year ago, Mum bought me an inflatable mattress so I could invite friends for sleepovers. The mattress is still in its original packaging.

'Come here.' Mum tries to kiss my cheek, but I push her away. I'm not in a cuddly mood right now. I'm in a sand-pouches-throwing mood. Or I would be if I still had the vest. Alex's words ring in my ears: *Hey, Sailor, what's with the life jacket? Afraid the bus will sink?*

I'm not sure which nickname I hate more: Sailor or Spy.

Mum and I go back to the bin to retrieve the vest. She's upset with me for throwing it away and makes me pull it out myself. The sickly sweetness of rotten bananas fills my nose. I gag and have to hold my breath as I reach in.

'We'll have to take it to the dry cleaner straight away,' Mum declares, holding the vest away from her between her fingers. It's covered with ketchup and crumbs. She slips it into a plastic bag and rubs sanitiser on her hands.

The lady at the dry cleaner gives us a confused look when she sees the vest. It seems there's no cleaning category for therapeutic apparel. She and Mum agree on 'sleeveless padded jacket'.

'When will it be ready?' Mum asks.

'For such a … um … *specialist* item it might take a week. I'm sorry.'

A week without having to wear the vest and cement my new nickname? *I'm* not sorry at all.

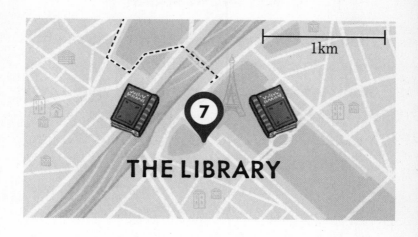

THE LIBRARY

I push open the wooden door of the public library. The smell of old books fills the air. It's a strange scent, a bit like vanilla, which I learned from my favourite science show is because of a chemical called lignin that breaks down as books age.

I sit down at a wooden reading table. Each table has an old-fashioned lamp with a green lampshade. The light they cast is soft. Except for the creaking wooden floors and shuffling of paper, it is completely silent.

The library is one of my favourite places in the world. It's not that I love reading books so much as I love collecting information.

I come here every Tuesday after school ends early at 12.15 p.m. It only takes me twelve minutes to walk here from home, and it was the very first place I was allowed to come to by myself. Now I come whenever I like – so long as Mum, Dad or Zoé know. The library's map collection is impressive. It contains all sorts of maps: geographical maps with countries and cities, topographical maps with mountains and oceans, moon maps with craters. Today, I came to find out more about what Monsieur Portmann told us about the tunnels, quarries and bunker below Paris.

I take two books from the section about underground Paris to my reading desk. I learn that in the 18th century, limestone was taken out of the underground to build Paris's most famous buildings: *Notre Dame*, the *Louvre*, the *Place de la Concorde*. Slowly but surely, the underground became so full of holes that it resembled Swiss cheese. But the thing is, if you create too many holes, building foundations become unstable. Nobody realised the risks of

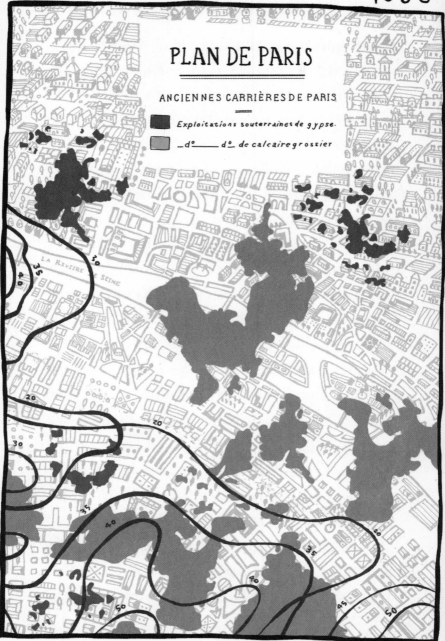

Echelle 1:60000

1908

PLAN DE PARIS

ANCIENNES CARRIÈRES DE PARIS

Exploitations souterraines de gypse.

_d°___ d°_ de calcaire grossier

LA RIVIÈRE DE SEINE

Les courbes bleues indiquent l'altitude de la surface superieure
du banc de roche qui sert général.^t de ciel aux exploitations de l'étage supér.^r

all that limestone being dug out and taken away – until a tunnel collapsed in 1774, swallowing an entire neighbourhood. That's when King Louis XVI finally appointed an architect called Charles-Axel Guillaumot to stabilise and map the quarries. Guillaumot set up the Inspection Générale des Carrières (IGC) to create maps of the underground.

I leaf through copies of the historical underground maps, the originals for which are over 200 years old. Eventually, I become aware that someone is watching me.

'Ah, the underground,' a woman says, coming to stand behind me. She wears her grey hair in a long, thick braid. 'Sorry to interrupt you. My name is Claudine. I work here. You come every Tuesday, right?'

I nod. 'From 2 to 4 p.m., yes. I'm Hugo.'

'And you're interested in the underground?'

'I guess so.'

'It's a magical place. I hung out there a lot back in the day. I'm too old for it now, though.'

'That's so cool! What's down there?' I ask.

Before Claudine can answer, a man across the table tells us to be quiet. Claudine gives me a sign to follow her out of the reading room, to a small office at the end of the corridor. Inside she opens a grey metallic drawer and takes out a map made of ten laminated pages. She tiles the pages together on a desk.

'Here. This is how the underground looks today,' Claudine says. 'The ones in the library are historical.'

Assembled together, the pages make up a giant map. It shows a surface plan of Paris traced in grey, with its buildings and boulevards, its parks and churches. Then there's the below-the-surface Paris – the Paris this map is really about. A mess of black, blue, orange and red, of circles, lines and rings. Sometimes the networks above and below align; at other points the underground follows different laws. I see tunnelled streets that twist and turn. There are connections between tunnels marked as 'chatière', meaning 'cat flap'. There are dead-end streets.

The map indicates different levels of depth, connected to each other through staircases and wells with ladders, reminding me of the *Jardin des Plantes*. Details like 'very low', 'flooded', 'collapsing ceiling' or 'impassable' appear next to the tunnels.

'Who made this?' I ask. I've never seen anything like it. This is the entire underground – over 250 kilometres of tunnels and caves according to Monsieur Portmann – elegantly compressed into one single square metre.

'A group of cataphiles,' Claudine answers.

'What are cataphiles?'

'Underground explorers. People aren't allowed to go down there. It's illegal. But it's so wonderful underground that some do anyway – like I used to. It's important for people going down there to have good maps.' Claudine's face lights up as she talks, making her look younger. 'Have you heard about Philibert Aspairt? she asks.

'No.' I say. I've only studied a couple of maps so far.

'He was the doorkeeper to the *Val-de-Grâce* military hospital. He got lost in 1793 while trying to steal wine from an underground cellar. There were no torches at the time, so when Philibert's candle went out, it was the end for him. They found his skeleton eleven years later. Next to it was a bottle of chartreuse.'

'That's horrible!' I imagine Philibert's skeleton all alone in the underground, the wine cellar keys slowly rusting on his belt. 'Why didn't he drink the bottle? It would have kept him alive longer.'

'That's one of many mysteries surrounding the story. It's said that he etched his initials into the glass – like an epitaph. The bottle hasn't been seen since,' Claudine continues. 'Philibert is our patron saint. The first thing cataphiles do when we go underground is visit his grave. But there is so much more to discover down there, and it's always changing. Every time it does, people tell me so that I can edit the maps and keep them up to date.'

The tiny hairs on my arms stand upright. I've wanted to be many things when I grow up – including a librarian. But to be the guardian of the underground maps on top of that?

I gaze at Claudine in a whole new light.

'But why would anything change down there?' I ask. 'I thought the underground had stayed the same since Guillaumot fortified everything?'

'Because of floods and small collapses. And don't forget, the authorities continue to close down certain access points because they don't want people to enter. In turn, the cataphiles open up new routes and find new ways to get in. It's a never-ending game of cat and mouse. And it's a lot of fun.' Claudine finishes with a mischievous grin.

The whole time she's been talking, I've been scanning the map. Now, without her knowing, I have the whole thing memorised. Each turn of a tunnel. Each cave. Each well.

'Here's the location of Philibert's grave,' Claudine says, pointing at the map below *Rue*

Henri Barbusse, in the *5th arrondissement*.

'I know that street! It's where my favourite restaurant is! *Brasserie Splendid*. How do you get into the underground from there?' I ask, excited by the idea.

'There's an access point here, through the manhole on *Boulevard Saint-Michel*.' She points at a spot on the map that says 'porte vers le ciel', meaning 'door to the sky'. I've never seen a more poetic expression for a manhole.

Claudine frowns suddenly, snatching her finger away as if she can undo what I've already seen (and memorised). 'Why do you ask? You're not planning on going underground, are you?' All her enthusiasm has faded now, and she looks older again.

'I'm just curious,' I say. The truth is, I'm more than just curious. A plan is taking shape in my mind.

'Good!' She breathes a sigh of relief. 'It really is dangerous down there. Remember what happened to Philibert! And you're right, *Brasserie Splendid* is a splendid restaurant.'

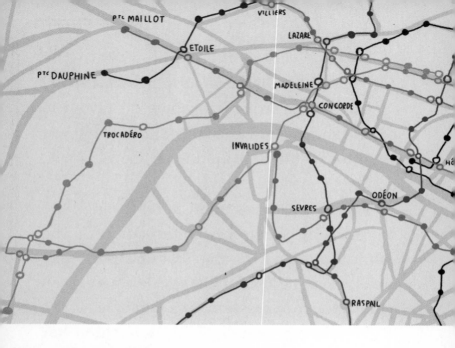

She laughs and I join in.

We often go to *Brasserie Splendid* for
Sunday lunch. It's my favourite restaurant,
for two very different reasons. First, they
have the best Dame Blanche in all of Paris:
vanilla ice cream with whipped cream and
warm Belgian chocolate sauce. And second,
there is a 1935 map of the Paris Métro on
the wall. The Métro looked very different
back then. In my mind, I like to superimpose
both maps, the one from 1935 and today's
map, and see what has changed. Sometimes,

I'm so consumed by this activity that my Dame Blanche melts away before I can eat it. Thinking of that map, my eyes return to the one on the table. I look at the 'door to the sky' next to *Brasserie Splendid*.

'How do you open a manhole cover, anyway?' I wonder, almost to myself.

'Hugo! All these questions! Promise me you're not planning a trip to the underground. I mean it. Besides, the answer is you would never manage to open a manhole cover by yourself. Not without a crowbar.' She seems to realise that she might have said too much again. 'And even then it would be *much* too heavy,' she adds quickly. 'Understood?'

'Do you ever dream of going back underground?' I ask, partly so I can avoid lying to her. But also because I wonder how it feels for her, updating these maps and not being able to use them herself.

Claudine takes the map pieces and puts them back into the drawer.

'Every day,' she admits. 'The bottle of chartreuse that Philibert tried to steal in 1793 is still down there somewhere. There's talk about a secret wine cellar. It's every cataphile's dream to find it, and the bottle. I tried many times but I never managed it. It's my biggest regret. The person who finds that bottle will be the hero of the cataphile community, that's for sure.'

'Would the chartreuse still be good after all those years?'

'Technically, yes. But they say the bottle is cursed: whoever opens it will perish in the underground. I don't believe that to be true, but no cataphile would ever open it out of respect for Philibert.'

'What do you miss most about the underground itself?' I ask, as Claudine locks the metal drawer. Is that my signal to stop talking? Am I bothering her now? I quickly check her face. She's smiling and her eyes are sparkling. These are all good signs according to what Mathilde has taught me.

'You know, Hugo,' Claudine says eventually, looking down at her feet as if she can see the underground between them, 'down there, nobody judges you. Up here, we're all so busy fussing about our differences. But in the underground, we're united by a common passion. Everyone is the same. It's that shared cataphile spirit that I miss most, I think.'

That night, I can't sleep. Not because I have to deal with my usual anxieties about being sucked into a black hole where time and space no longer exist. But because I can't stop thinking about Claudine's map and the cataphile spirit. And about the secret wine cellar with Philibert Aspairt's bottle of chartreuse.

All I would have to do is find that bottle, and I'd be welcomed into the cataphile community.

The question is: could I find it?

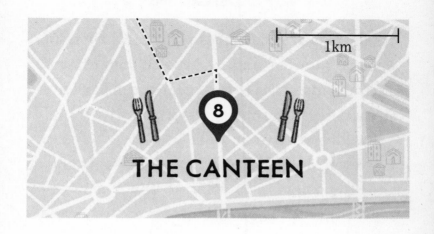

THE CANTEEN

The girl standing next to Julie is called Nina. She's on the swimming team, and she's also the editor of the school newspaper. Both are ahead of me in the lunch line.

Nina has really long red hair that covers her shoulders. Currently it's wet like Julie's. When she throws it back, a couple of water droplets land on my lenses, blurring my vision. I take my sunglasses off despite the bright lights.

Long after Julie and Nina have sat down, I carry my tray to an empty table next to a window where I always sit. Alone. But then I think about the friendship discussion with Mathilde. 'Practise', she had said.

I put down my tomato pasta. Now is as good a time as any. Julie still hasn't said anything about the letter and it's been five days already.

I walk over to their table.

'Hello.' I look down at Julie, trying to appear positive and relaxed. But inside my chest my heart is pounding. According to the social story cards, it's best to keep eye contact with the other person for at least a third of the discussion. I don't know how long this conversation will last, so that won't be easy to regulate. More is probably better than less, so I focus on Julie's face.

'Hi?' Julie says, like it's a question.

'It's great to see you,' I say, remembering the importance of politeness. Julie and Nina smile at each other. This is going well. *'Talking to people is fun!'* The words of a particular card pop into my mind. *'I can ask someone about their favourite things.'*

'What's your favourite thing these days?' I ask. 'Aside from swimming, I mean.'

Julie pushes her chair back a little. Maybe I've invaded her private space? The cards suggest standing an arm's length away from the other person, so I quickly adjust my position.

'I don't know,' Julie replies. 'I don't have that much free time, what with swimming and all.' She looks at Nina as if she has a better answer. Nina shrugs.

'You swim well,' I compliment her, because giving compliments makes people happy. 'You've broken a lot of school records. That's cool.'

'Uh, thanks,' she mumbles.

Now, according to the cards, Julie should ask me about *my* favourite things. But she doesn't.

'Should I tell you what I like?' I offer.

'I guess so, yeah.'

Why does she keep looking at Nina like that? I'm the one talking to her. She should make eye contact. According to Mathilde, that's how you can tell someone's interested in the conversation.

I continue anyway.

'You already know that I like maps. I have this new book called *Transit Maps of the World*. It has rail maps, metro maps, all kinds of maps. My favourite is the London Underground because it looks like an abstract painting.

'And did you know that Doha in Qatar has one of the fastest driverless metro systems in the world? It can go up to 100 kilometres per hour. That's very impressive when you compare it to the Paris driverless line with a maximum speed of eighty kilometres per hour.'

My hands start to flap, like they always do when I really love talking about something or when I get overwhelmed by the world. I quickly hide them in my pockets.

'Um, cool …' Julie says, again glancing at Nina. Nina's face is hidden by her hair as she stares down at the table – although I'm not sure at what.

'I can show you the book, if you like?' I suggest. 'The pictures are great.'

'Maybe another time. Like I said, I'm very busy with swimming practice these days.' Julie checks her wristwatch. 'Nina, I think we're running late for – you know. That thing.' Julie stands abruptly, downing the rest of her drink.

'Oh yeah ... that thing ...' Nina slowly repeats.

I start to panic. First of all, according to the cards, I should be the one ending the conversation by saying 'goodbye'. And secondly, this cannot be over yet. There's still stuff I want to say.

'What kind of thing is it?' I ask, buying time, still trying to make eye contact.

Julie puts her drink down loudly. 'Can you *please* stop staring at me? It's making me uncomfortable.'

She's no longer smiling. She's moved away, beyond the arm's length suggested by the cards. That's not good.

'I'm sorry,' I say. 'It's probably been more than a third of the conversation. It's difficult to keep track.'

'What are you talking about?' Nina snaps.

There's still time to make Julie smile again.

Ask questions. Tell jokes. Give compliments. Maybe I should ask about her Siamese cat. People love talking about their pets. I know that because Aunt Mafalda, Mum's sister, had a couple of aquatic turtles called Cleo and Caesar, and we stopped visiting her for a while because they were all she talked about. It drove Dad crazy.

'How's your cat?' I ask.

'What is this? Some kind of interview? You're freaking me out.' Julie spins away. 'Come on, Nina. Let's go.'

'I like the colour of your skirt!' I add, in a last attempt.

Nina shoots me a fierce look. 'Stalker!'

Note to self: don't mention clothing or colour thereof.

'Julie, did you get my letter?'

Julie stops and turns to Nina. 'Go ahead, I'll catch up with you.'

She comes back towards me, and I can't catch her gaze. It's like she's looking right through me. Suddenly I don't want to hear her answer. I don't think it's going to be the one I want.

'Look,' she says, 'I've moved on.'

'Where to?' I ask. But my heart is pounding loudly enough to say I know exactly what she means.

'I mean we're not friends anymore, Hugo. I'm sorry I have to tell you like this. I hoped you would just understand the signs – but of course you wouldn't. You're …' She stops.

'I'm what?' My cheeks burn. Why am I still asking question when the answers hurt so much?

'Different.'

'You mean weird. Too weird for you, is that it?'

Julie doesn't answer.

I didn't know I could feel so many emotions at once. Disappointment. Anger. Sadness. They wash over me like a huge wave. I'm trying to stay afloat, but I don't know for how long I'll manage.

'Did you read my letter?' I repeat.

'I did,' she says. 'The Allosaurus and all. It was nice. But that's not who I am anymore. I've changed. I'm sorry.'

As she turns and leaves, I take the social story cards out of my pocket. I shuffle through them, but I already know that none match this outcome. What went wrong?

I look up again to see if anyone was watching. But they're all too absorbed in their groups, clustered together like grapes with their backs turned towards me.

I'm like that single grape that gets left in the punnet. I'm not part of any cluster.

Claudine's words come into my mind: *Down there, nobody judges you. Up here, we're all so busy fussing about our differences. But in the underground, we're united by a common passion.*

Maybe I'm not meant to be a grape at all. Grapes thrive in the sunlight. I prefer the shade, like a blackberry, or even the dark, like a peanut. Most people don't know that peanuts are a fruit, but they are. Botanically, anyway. They just thrive underground.

Maybe I would too.

The idea germinates in an instant. Questions sprout. And I decide I can't wait until Tuesday to find the answers ...

THE LIBRARY
(AGAIN)

Claudine is at her desk, unpacking a large box of books. The smell of fresh print fills my nose. When she sees me, her face lights up.

'Hugo! What brings you here on a Thursday afternoon? You usually come on Tuesdays.'

'2 to 4 p.m., yes,' I say. 'But I have more questions.'

'About the underground? I don't think that's a good idea, Hugo. I told you, it's too dangerous for you to go down there.'

'This is for a project,' I say, hoping that she'll assume it's for school and that I won't have to lie.

I'm terrible at lying. I tried telling Mum I had a stomach bug once to get out of going to school, but it felt so wrong that I spent twice as long confessing to the lie as I had telling it, and Mum already knew anyway. She says that when I lie, I forget to blink.

Claudine checks her watch.

'I have a fifteen-minute break I can take. Follow me.'

She takes me back to the small office at the end of the corridor.

'Have a seat,' she says, waving to the visitor's chair. 'What do you want to know?'

'About mechanoreceptors.'

Claudine blinks. 'What?'

'Our biology teacher told us about a lab below the *Jardin des Plantes*. A scientist imported insects from above the surface to see how they would develop in the underground.'

'I've never heard anything about an underground lab. It sounds interesting.'

'It is. The insects lost their sense of sight, but their mechanoreceptors grew. Do you think that would happen to humans too? Do you think our senses would somehow change?'

Claudine throws her head back and laughs. 'I think you would have to spend years in the underground for that to happen! Why do you ask?'

'I'm just curious.' And I needed an excuse to talk to her.

'Well, I don't know about the insects, but it takes people a while to get used to the complete silence down there,' Claudine continues. 'It makes some people anxious. It's a very unusual experience.'

'I like the quiet.'

'Me too,' Claudine smiles. 'I guess that's why I became a librarian. But sometimes even the library is too noisy for me. And then there's the commute here. I hate the Métro! The brake noise gets me every time.'

'I know what you mean,' I agree, nodding. 'And the smell.'

'So greasy.'

'Dusty and metallic.'

'With a dash of burnt rubber,' Claudine adds.

'That's a very accurate description.' Claudine reminds me of me – not exactly the same, but if Claudine found her people underground, I'm even more convinced that I can too.

'But tell me more about the underground lab,' she continues, before asking the same question I asked Monsieur Portmann: 'How did they get in from the *Jardin des Plantes*?'

That's my cue.

'Through an old well, apparently.' I try to sound casual. 'How did *you* get into the underground?'

Claudine frowns. 'How does that relate to your project about the insects?'

'My project isn't only about the underground lab. It's about the underground in general.' I remind myself to blink.

Claudine hesitates for a second, but then she opens the metallic drawer. She takes out the laminated underground map and lays it out on the desk, just like she did two days ago. I hold my breath.

'There are entrances all over Paris. A popular one is the *Petite Ceinture*,' Claudine says, taking out another, smaller map.

I try to hide my excitement.

'It's an abandoned railway built more than 150 years ago,' she explains. 'It circles the city – hence the name 'the little belt'. When the Métro became more and more popular, the *Petite Ceinture* was abandoned. Today it's overgrown with weeds, but certain parts are

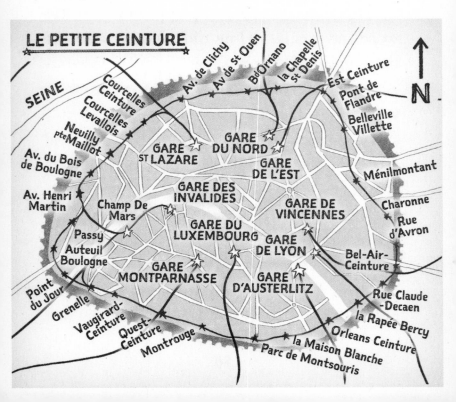

open to the public as walking trails. Back in the day, we used to enter through this tunnel here.' Claudine points at an abandoned railway station in the southern part of the city.

That's it! That's my way in!

Claudine instantly crushes my hope.

'This part of the railway isn't open to the public anymore. It's fenced off and there are hefty fines if you get caught trying to cross it. Plus it's not in the safest area.'

'Isn't there an easier way to get into the underground?' I can't hide my disappointment, and it makes Claudine frown. 'I mean,' I search for something to say: something that isn't a lie but isn't suspicious. 'I mean, if it's so difficult, I'm amazed you ever got in.'

'It isn't meant to be easy, Hugo. A trip to the underground is something that you earn. If you can't find a way in, it means you're not ready yet.'

But I *am* ready! I almost say it out loud.

'How do *non*-cataphiles get in?' I wonder. 'Legally, I mean?'

'Other than the underground police or sewer

workers? You need an official permit from the Inspection Générale des Carrières, which you can only get if you're a grown-up on some geological mission.'

Well, I might not be a grown-up, but I am on a mission.

Generally speaking, I obey the rules. They give me a sense of safety in an otherwise chaotic universe. In this case, however, it looks like I will have to make an exception.

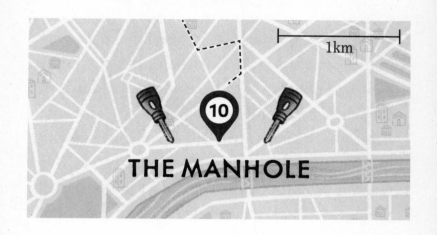

THE MANHOLE

I've never sneaked out of the house before. I've never wanted to. I hate breaking rules. The discomfort is like an itch I can't scratch until I stop what I'm doing or confess it. This time the discomfort of doing nothing is stronger.

Mum is snoring (something she denies ever doing). Dad is away in Australia on a business trip. Zoé's room is silent. As I tiptoe through the hallway, the floor makes a creaking sound. I freeze. Was that Mum getting out of bed? Seconds later, I hear her snoring again. Feeling guilty but determined, I open the front door and quickly sneak out of our apartment.

It's 5.30 a.m. and still dark as I make my way to *Brasserie Splendid.* I've never been outside at this time of morning. Especially not alone. I'm surprised and relieved by how busy Paris is at this hour. Rubbish trucks are rolling in ahead of the weekend. Seafood is being delivered. Two women are practising Tai Chi in the park. All this activity makes me forget my fear. *You're not really alone,* I tell myself.

I take a deep breath and walk faster. It should take me twenty minutes. I have to cross the *Seine* from the Right Bank where we live to the Left Bank where *Brasserie Splendid* is located. Another first for me: I have never walked across the river at night. The water level is high and glitters blackly.

When I reach it, *Brasserie Splendid's* illuminated sign reflects on the wet pavement. It's been raining for two days in a row. Despite this, the small round tables and their matching rattan chairs are lined up on the pavement outside. Already, the air is filling with the smell of oysters and bleach. In an hour the first customers will show up for their café au lait and croissant. A little drizzle never discouraged a true Parisian from taking their breakfast outside.

I have to be home by 7 a.m., when Mum wakes up. This is just a reconnaissance mission. Before I show up at the manhole, fully equipped and ready to go underground, I need to make sure I know how to open it. Yesterday I found a thick, flat screwdriver in our basement where my dad keeps his toolbox. I have no idea what he does with it – he's never even changed a light bulb. Mum is in charge of everything.

I kneel down on the wet pavement and take a deep breath, sliding the screwdriver into the cover keyhole. It's heavy – much *much* heavier than I thought it would be. Even with all my weight pushing the handle of the screwdriver down, and bouncing my knee against the back of my hand, I can barely lift the cover. I definitely can't push it to one side. Each time I tire of holding it up a fraction, it falls heavily back into place with a *thunk*! Soon I'm breathing hard and the heel of my hand feels bruised and sore.

'I need more leverage,' I mutter, wiping my damp forehead.

'Hugo?'

I jump to my feet, hiding the screwdriver. I turn and recognise Pierre, a young waiter from *Brasserie Splendid*.

'Is that you?' he says. A box of fresh oysters almost slips out of his hands as he moves closer to make sure that it really is me. 'What are you doing here at this time of day?'

'Don't tell my parents!' I say. It's the first thing that pops into my mind. Pierre knows Mum and Dad well, and he loves them because they always leave him a generous tip.

'I won't.' Pierre frowns. 'But you should be careful. We get a lot of weirdos around here after hours. They use that manhole to go underground.'

'You mean the cataphiles,' I correct him. 'They're not weirdos. They're just different. Certainly nothing to be scared of.'

Pierre lowers his voice. 'What about the Green Devil?'

'Who?'

'The Green Devil! He's been haunting the underground for centuries. They say he dines on the flesh of children. He takes them to his cave and eats them alive.'

'... You're just saying this to scare me, aren't you?'

'I am,' Pierre says with a grin. 'But every legend has some truth. That's why they exist – to prevent kids like you from doing stupid things.'

'I won't do anything stupid,' I say. And I'm not lying. Going underground isn't stupid. Not if you're well prepared – and you have all the maps stored in your head.

'Good. Then I'll see you for Dame Blanche next Sunday?' Pierre places the oysters one by one on a bed of shaved ice in one of the stalls outside *Brasserie Splendid*.

It's time to leave. The pavement is slowly filling with people. I can't carry on tampering with the manhole cover now. But I'm not giving up. The world where I belong is only a manhole cover or a railway track away.

One way or another, I *will* find a way in.

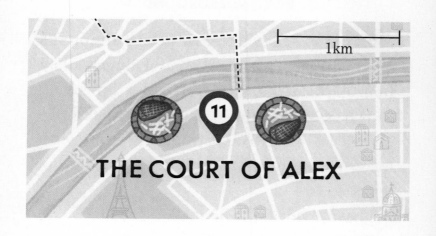

THE COURT OF ALEX

Alex is holding court at a large table in the canteen. He's surrounded by kids from our class. Julie's there too. She gives me a nod when she notices me looking, then turns away. That's all I will get from her now. A nod. A nod that says: 'You're not a total stranger to me, but don't talk to me anymore. We're not friends.'

I sit alone and play with my steak frites. Just as I'm about to take a bite, I see Alex getting up from his throne. His voice raises so that I – and everyone else – can hear it, and every comic book sound effect he makes.

'*Bam!* He attacked me. He grabbed my wrist and threw me to the floor. I got up immediately to counter-attack, piercing his chest with my bare hand. *Pow!* I almost killed him – *Mortal Kombat* style.' Alex talks fast, as if he's commentating a boxing match. He makes an expansive, circling gesture with his arms, supposed to look like some kind of martial art.

I have no idea who he's talking about.

'With your bare hand?' Enzo asks, breathless.

'It's called nukite: the spear-hand.' Alex narrows his eyes and extends his fingers, tightly pressed together to demonstrate. He makes a sudden thrusting movement, stabbing thin air. 'It's a secret karate move. Deadly and *very* difficult to master. I could be arrested just for telling you about it.'

'Woooow,' Enzo breathes again. 'And it was definitely the Green Devil?'

I choke on a piece of steak. The Green Devil, again?

'... super scary,' Alex is saying now, answering another follower's question. 'And super strong. Check this out.' Alex pulls up the sleeves of his jumper to reveal a large violet bruise on his forearm.

Enzo is wide-eyed. 'He did that to you?'

Alex nods.

'No, he didn't,' I interrupt, unable to stay quiet about this obvious lie. 'That's from when you fell over at the park the other week. I saw it.'

'Shut up, Spy!' Alex barks. His cheeks are red. 'This,' he points at the bruise, re-addressing his audience, 'is from the Green Devil.'

'Really?' Julie asks. It's clear that she doesn't believe him either. 'From what I know, the Green Devil lives in the underground.'

'Well guess what?' Alex says smugly. 'I found an entrance to the catacombs in our basement. I went down there last night.'

Everyone gasps – including me. He's talking about the underground. *My* place. It's as if two separate parts of my life have just overlapped, like the above and below layers of Paris in Claudine's map. And I already know that there are entrances to the underground all over Paris. I read up on them after Claudine told me about the *Petite Ceinture*. Alex could be telling the truth about there being one in his basement. This could be my third way to get into the underground!

'Isn't that dangerous?' someone asks.

Alex shrugs dismissively. 'I like to live dangerously. After my counter-attack, the Green Devil retreated. But he'll be back, and so will I. This wasn't our last fight. It was only the beginning.' Now Alex sounds like a voice-over from a film trailer.

Julie snorts. 'I've been in your basement, remember? So has–' She glances at me, then away. 'How come I never saw any entrance to the underground?'

Alex shrugs. 'It was hidden behind some junk my mum wants to sell. I had to take pictures of it, and when I moved it, I saw the hole. Deep. Dark. *Mysterious.*'

'How far down did you go?' I wonder.

'Far enough,' he says.

I know Alex's basement better than Julie does. We used to go there every time I visited him because that's where his mum kept his bike. I couldn't ride very well at the time, so I'd watch Alex circle the tiny courtyard of their apartment building. Sometimes I'd name random car models and he had to make the sound of the engine with his mouth as he braked and cornered. It was fun.

A neighbour gave the bike to Alex as a hand-me-down, and it was the most expensive thing he owned. I don't know much about Alex's family, but I do know that he lives alone with his mum in a tiny apartment and that they don't have much money. I know that there's no key to their basement. Only a combination lock. And I know the combination to that lock: 1789. The year of the French Revolution.

'How cold was it down there?' I ask.

'Freezing!' Alex shivers at the memory. He's only answering my questions because it helps his performance, but I'd better wear my winter coat just in case.

'Then there were the rats ...'

I frown at this. 'Rats live in the sewers, not the catacombs. The catacombs are where they stored bones. There's nothing for rats to eat there. Unlike in the sewers.'

'How do you know, Sailor?' Alex demands. 'Have you been? I hope you took your life jacket! I hear there's water down there.' His words prompt another chorus of laughter from his followers. I shield myself from it with facts.

'And when you say "catacombs" what you really mean is *quarries*.' I know this because Alex lives on the Left Bank. That's where most of the limestone quarry network fans out. 'A lot of people mistakenly refer to the whole underground as the catacombs, but that's only a tiny part of it. Remember what Monsieur Portmann told us when we went to the *Jardin des Plantes*?'

'Shut up!' Alex barks. 'What do you know about it?'

'I've seen the maps,' I say. I know each and every tunnel and chatière on Claudine's map.

I've memorised the entire maze. More than that, I know about Philibert's tombstone and the secret wine cellar.

'Maps are for wimps,' Alex declares, raising his fist. 'Real adventure comes without safety nets.' And now he sounds like a fortune cookie.

'You know what they'll write on your tombstone, Spy? *Maps were his only friends!*' I look at Julie. She looks away. Their laughter washes over me like a tsunami. My ears ring with it. The fluorescent lights are getting brighter. I put on my sunglasses. Anger bubbles in my stomach like lava. Blood pulses in my cheeks.

The canteen is receding around me: the ceiling, the floor, the steak frites right in front of me. Even the stink of bleach and floor wax has begun to fade. I have become my rage, red hot and urgent, and I'm moments away from throwing my plastic lunch tray at Alex.

If only I had my vest now.

Then I remember what Mathilde taught me: 'When you're about to erupt like a volcano,' she says, 'take ten deep breaths and count backwards from ten.'

I close my eyes. Breathe.

Ten.

Nine.

Eight …

It's not working. There's only one thing left to do.

My chair tips as I storm out of the canteen, rushing past tray carts with half-eaten slices of pizza and leftover pasta. I head straight for the little room next to my classroom. It has one desk with two chairs, and three more stacked in the corner. I ignore them and slide onto the red beanbag that is mine alone. I close my eyes, focussing on the darkness behind my eyelids. I feel the silence around me from the empty classrooms.

This is what it must be like in the underground. Quiet. Dark. Peaceful.

A perfect habitat.

THE FISHING SECTION

It's Saturday, and the local outdoor sports shop has everything I need. Alex was right about one thing: there is water in the underground. I've seen pictures. There's water and mud – lots of it.

'Going on a fishing trip?' the cashier asks as he scans items from my shopping bag. Hip waders. *Beep.* A waterproof rucksack, a compass and a head torch. *Beep. Beep. Beep.* A pack of ten protein bars – this won't be cheap. I had to empty my piggybank. There was over a hundred euros in there from Christmas and birthdays.

I nod in answer to the cashier's question.

His name is Ben according to his tag. His face is covered by a large beard.

'Where to?' Ben asks. Blood rushes to my cheeks. I try to think of somewhere but my brain is empty.

'I-it's a secret,' I stutter eventually. After all, a lot of fishermen keep their best fishing spots to themselves – that's what Dad told me.

'A secret river twenty metres below Paris?' Ben chuckles. 'We've got plenty of cataphiles among our customers. They all pretend they're going fishing, but I can always tell what they're really up to from what they're buying – or not buying. Fishing rods? Bait? Never. Only hip waders and head torches. I guess there aren't many fish in the underground.'

'I guess not.' I don't know where to look. Will he report me to the police?

Ben leans over the counter ominously, and I'm on edge enough to lean back. 'Watch out for the Green Devil,' he says.

'But that's just a legend, isn't it?' I ask, unable to take my eyes off his beard.

Ben laughs. 'Of course, it is! But the underground is a dangerous place even without the Green Devil. A few years ago, a couple of teenagers went down there and got lost. Took them three days to find an exit. I take it you'll have a guide with you?'

He means a person, an adult – but a guide can also be a book or a document. A guide can be a map.

'Yes,' I say, nodding eagerly, relieved that I don't have to lie. 'Yes, I'll have a guide with me.'

'Do they have waders?'

'Ugh … I don't think so …' Also true.

'You want to go grab another pair just in case? You can always return them, just keep the receipt. You get twenty-eight days.'

I'm nodding, already wandering back to the waders. I pick a size at random. I hope I have enough money for all this.

'There you go,' says Ben. 'Do you need a bag?'

I put my change away and take it. I did have enough money – barely.

'No thank you,' I say, stuffing everything inside my rucksack.

'You're welcome.' Ben leans over the counter again, bringing his beard closer. 'And be careful.'

I leave the shop and meet Zoé as she crosses the road from one opposite. She eyes my rucksack, now bulging slightly, and opens her mouth to say something.

'Did you find what you were looking for?' I ask quickly. I'm running out of excuses for why I wanted to tag along to the local shops only to look at 'boring sports stuff'.

'Oh! Yeah.' Zoé beams, instantly forgetting her curiosity. 'Look, I got this cool new laptop bag. You like it?' She holds up a laptop bag made of a smooth material that makes me think of scuba suits – except that the laptop bag is striped with a pineapple pattern.

'It's great,' I say. But now that I've got my supplies, my mind is already in the underground.

On our way home, we pass a bookstore. In

its window, I see the cover of a graphic novel showing a long green hand creeping out of a manhole. The title, written in neon green letters, jumps off the page: THE GREEN DEVIL.

I gulp down my fears. *It's only a legend,* I tell myself. *It's only a legend ...*

Mum is at her Sunday morning yoga class. Dad is in Japan trying to convince the Japanese that French champagne is better than their local rice wine.

And I'm standing outside Alex's apartment building with a rucksack full of waders, water bottles, peanut butter sandwiches and protein bars. Only it turns out that wasn't everything I needed after all. I've been so focussed on getting into the basement and from the basement into the underground that I've forgotten a third access problem: how am I going to get into the building?

Access requires a code. In this case it's a letter followed by a four-digit number. If I don't enter the correct code, the front door won't open.

I type in the last code I remember Alex using: D6634. Nothing. I'm not surprised. Access codes get changed regularly. And it's been 262 days since we last hung out.

There's nothing I can do but wait, until a man with a wheeled shopping trolley stops in front of the door. I watch him type in the code B4905. Then B4950. Then, muttering to himself, B4955. *Bzzzz.* The door pops open.

'Let me help you with that,' I say, lifting the man's trolley up a small step in front of the door. I follow him through into a hall lined with silver post boxes. Just like that, I'm in. Mosaic tiles cover the floor. The air smells of detergent.

I head straight to the basement area, down the old stone steps of the staircase. Yellow light illuminates the dingy corridor at the bottom, and several shorter offshoots. Every apartment has its own small basement, one next to the other, and all of them are protected by metal gates. Alex's basement is on the right. Soon I'm standing right in front of it. The moment I see the lock, my heart drops. Someone has changed it from a combination padlock to one with a key. I shake the gate even though I know it won't do any good. Once again, I'm so close yet so far from my destination.

'What are you doing here?'

I'm surprised I didn't smell her before she spoke. She smells salty-sweet and acrid. A strange blend of chicken broth and cold cigarette smoke. It makes me gag as I turn around.

She wears an old-fashioned flowery apron. Her teeth have a large gap in the middle. We French call this 'les dents du bonheur', or 'happiness teeth'. But there's nothing happy about this scowling old lady.

'I ... was just checking on something someone told me about. It's in his basement. But it's locked.'

I'm not lying, but I can tell that she doesn't care. She sucks air through the gap in her teeth, making a wet, *tsk*ing sound.

'I don't like strangers roaming around.'

'I'm not a stranger,' I insist. 'Alex is my – I know the owner from school.'

'Then he can show you whatever it is himself. Now get out of here.'

'Excuse me, but who are you?'

'*Who am I?*' she echoes, her voice high-pitched. '*I* am Madame Ginette, the concierge of this building for the past thirty years – and the one who will call the police if you don't get out of here *right now*!'

I flee, taking the steps two at a time. The rucksack thumps solidly against my back.

Manhole covers that can't be opened. A railway line that's closed to the public. Padlocks without a key.

Will I ever get into the underground?

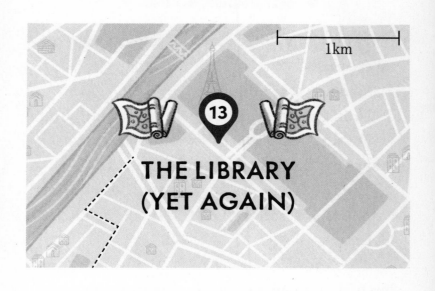

THE LIBRARY (YET AGAIN)

We were talking about the French Revolution in school this morning. The French Revolution was a time in history when the French people decided to get rid of their king because he and his family lived in a palace with a special room just for their dogs, while the rest of the country was starving to death.

After class I approach Alex by his locker. It's plastered with skateboard stickers and a logo for BeeRocs, the trainers everyone seems to be wearing now. Mum bought me a pair, too, but I struggle with the laces. I'm not good at tying knots in general; it's to do with my 'fine motor skills'.

'What do you want, Spy?'

'Nothing!' My voice comes out higher than I want it to. 'The French Revolution just always makes me think about your basement.'

'What are you talking about?' Alex asks, wrestling his battered history book inside his locker.

'You know – 1789. The year of the French Revolution. The code to your basement.'

'Not anymore,' Alex says. 'You need a key now.'

'Oh, really?' I hope he can't hear my heart beating as loudly as I can. 'That's a good idea. Combination locks can be cracked. There are only 10,000 possible combinations for a four-digit code using 0 to 9 – fewer if you don't repeat numbers. Keyed locks are safer. You just need to make sure you keep the key safe – and any spares. I hope you're not keeping yours anywhere obvious, like under the doormat or a flower–'

Alex slams the locker door shut, cutting me off. He turns and stares at me. I can't decide the appropriate level of blinking.

'Don't even think about it, Spy.'

Blink. 'Think about what?' *Blink.*

'I know you, remember? We used to be – we used to hang out.'

I nod. 'Yes. In fact, the last time was in your basement, 263 days ago.'

'Well you can forget about my basement, and the entrance to the catacombs. It's way too dangerous down there for a wimp like you. If the Green Devil doesn't get you, the rats will. You wouldn't last five minutes.'

'Who said anything about going down there?'

'You were thinking about it.'

'No, I wasn't!'

I'm practically squeaking now.

Alex smirks and slings his rucksack over his shoulder. '... 263 days later, Spy, and you still can't lie.'

He walks away then, and I'm glad for it. Even though I didn't find out where he keeps the key to the basement. He knows I can't lie, and how I try to get around it. If I'm like Superman, he's like Lex Luthor: he knows my kryptonite.

It's only Monday and I'm back at the library. I can't think about anything other than finding a way into the underground.

'Still working on your project?' Claudine appears behind me again.

I nod tiredly. For the past hour, I've been desperately looking for another entrance now that I can't get into Alex's basement. I haven't found one, and I've exhausted all the underground map books. The one currently open on my desk is about its history.

'Ah,' says Claudine, picking it up and leafing through it. 'This is a good one. Have you read about the bunker yet?'

'No,' I say. 'And I don't think I can read any more. My eyes are burning.'

Claudine pulls a chair from the desk next to me and sits down.

'Which school do you go to?' she asks suddenly. 'The *Lycée Montaigne*?'

'No, but my sister does. Why?'

'Because the bunker is underneath the *Lycée Montaigne*. The Luftwaffe – that was the German Air Force – they occupied it during World War II.'

'Underground?'

'Yes. A bomb-proof bunker underneath your sister's school. It's a strange thought, isn't it?'

Strange to think that the access to the underground I'm looking for might be right under my nose! Or at least right under my sister's nose.

'Zoé's never even mentioned it,' I marvel.

'She probably doesn't know,' Claudine replies.

'Oh. So you can't get to the bunker from the school?'

She shakes her head 'It's sealed off. Just imagine what the kids would get up to if it wasn't!'

Claudine laughs, but I can't join in. It's another dead end.

'No,' Claudine continues, 'entering the underground via the *Lycée Montaigne* is next to impossible. Except for the UX.'

OK. Maybe not a dead end.

'What's the UX?'

'You mean *who*,' Claudine corrects me, getting up and walking to the shelves nearest to us. 'Another interesting lead for your school project. The UX stands for Urban eXperiment. They're cataphiles of a special sort. In the early 1980s, when they were still just kids themselves, they broke into the Ministry of Telecommunications and stole maps of the underground. Since then, they've done amazing things. Like setting up a cinema under the *Trocadéro* and restoring parts of the underground that the government isn't interested in or doesn't have the money to maintain. Here, read this. You'll love it.'

She takes a book and hands it to me.

'An elite group of cataphiles? Can I talk to

them about my project? Where do I find them?'
I ask. My hands are flapping like I'm about to
take off and fly away, that's how excited I am.

'You can't find them. Nobody can – not even
the government. They find you if they want to.
Membership is by invitation only.'

'And you're a member, aren't you?'

'Secrecy is the hallmark of the UX,' Claudine
says with a wide grin. 'Even if I was, I couldn't
tell you.'

'So you are.'

Still grinning, Claudine stands and returns
her chair to the neighbouring desk. 'I need to
get back to work now. Good luck with your
research.' Then she disappears behind the
shelves.

I read the back cover of the book she gave me:

The fascinating history of Paris's most
secretive organisation. Its goal: to restore
the hidden and abandoned parts of Paris.
Its motto: **Ne cherchez pas** – Do not search.

That means do not search for *them*, I know. The UX is yet another elite group I'm excluded from joining, like the kids at the back of the bus. The ones picked first for team sports. The ones who actually get invited to birthday parties. Only this time I care.

I *want* to be part of this cataphile scene – more than anything. But if everything is secret and hidden and 'invitation only', how will they ever know that I exist? How can I even get down there when every access is locked?

Dejectedly, I return the book to its shelf. Walking back to my desk, I notice a flash of silver on the brown wooden floor. A paperclip. I pick it up, and an idea hits me with such clarity that I jump.

This is my key to the underground!

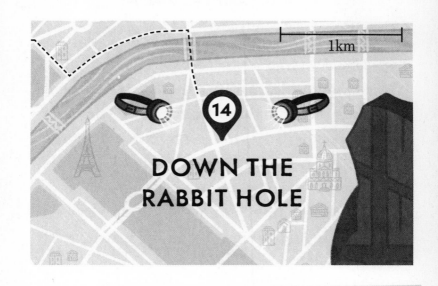

DOWN THE
RABBIT HOLE

Dear Mum, Dad and Zoé,

When you find this letter, don't worry. I'm fine. I'm somewhere dark and peaceful, where I won't have to wear my sunglasses and my noise-cancelling headphones. A place where everyone is the same — even me.

Please don't look for me. I'll return on my own when I've found what I'm looking for (which may take a while because no one knows where it is).

Until then, don't worry.

Love,

Hugo

The following day, I return to Alex's apartment building. I type in the entrance code. The main door opens with a soft buzz. The concierge apartment is just to the right. It has a window that looks into the building instead of out, allowing Madame Ginette to keep an eye on the coming and goings of tenants. I sneak past it and down into the basement, armed with two paper clips now.

I look around me. There's no one here. My hands tremble as I bend the first paper clip at a 45-degree angle. Then I pull the second one straight and pinch a kink into the end, copying a YouTube tutorial I watched last night. I insert both clips into the lock and wiggle the top one. Soft clicks inside the padlock will tell me if I'm doing this right.

I hear no clicks. The paper clips bend uselessly.

This isn't working.

I sigh.

A trip to the underground is something that you earn. If you can't find a way in, it means you're not ready yet.

Claudine's words return to my mind.

I shake the gate in frustration. I was too distracted to notice last time, but it's surprisingly light, rattling loudly. The hinges are like fingers of metal attached to the wall. They point up to the ceiling, spearing rings of metal attached to the gate. I rattle the gate again. The rings aren't even tight. What if, rather than picking the lock, I could just lift the gate off its hinges? Could it really be that simple?

After a few minutes of straining, I have my answer: no. Because 'surprisingly light' and 'light' are not the same thing. Before I can lift the gate high enough for the rings to clear the eight centimetres of metal fingers, I have to set it back down with a clunk to rest. Suddenly, I smell chicken broth.

Madame Ginette!

'Hello?' she calls.

My heart beats in my throat. With shaking hands, I seize the gate again and heave it upwards three centimetres, willing metal not to scrape against metal, willing myself not to groan.

'Who's there?'

Six centimetres.

'I warn you; I'll call the police.'

I stagger as I clear the remaining metal and the gate swings towards me, still padlocked to the other wall. Awkwardly I shimmy around until I have one hand on each side, then both hands on the other. I attempt to close it behind me by lifting it back onto its hinges. But I can't. I'll have to leave it pulled to.

She's close enough for me to hear her footsteps now.

I rush into the basement. The light of the corridor spills through just enough for me to see my way around without using the light switch on the wall. Where's the hole? I look around me. The basement is packed. I see boxes, chairs, cupboards, an old sewing machine with a wrought-iron base – but no hole. And any minute now Madame Ginette is going to see *me*.

'Hello?'

I dive behind a big black suitcase. There she is! From the other side of the gate, Madame Ginette peeks into the basement. I hold my breath. If she notices that the gate is off its hinges I'm done for. But she only *tsk*s, shakes her head, then shuffles away. I take a deep breath. My entire body is shaking, and I need a moment to calm down.

Opposite me is Alex's old bike.

Maybe it's because I'm so tense, but it brings back memories that make my eyes sting.

From the dust covering the bike, it looks like it's been here since the last time I came to see Alex. His legs were already too long for it then. His knees came up to his arms when he pedalled. He told me that he wanted a skateboard, but that they had no money to buy one. He told me that he wanted to hang out with the cool kids at school, the ones with the expensive trainers who did stunts at the park. I told him that for an autistic kid like me, cycling was already a challenge. Skateboarding was out of the question. It was the beginning of the end of our friendship.

I wipe my eyes and look away from the bike. That's when I see it. A gaping, ragged hole in the wall.

I wonder how many such entrances to the underground there are left – in cellars and church crypts and basements like this one. The Inspection Générale des Carrières, the authority in charge of the underground, has sealed off most of them. This one is less than a metre wide and so dark it's like a black hole leading to another dimension. I can't help staring at it.

And hesitating.

If this were a film or a book, it would be the scene where the hero stumbles upon a mysterious portal to another world – like Alice falling down the rabbit hole, or Dorothy being swept up by that tornado. They didn't have any friends with them either – unless you count Toto. Even Lucy went through the wardrobe on her own at first.

I can do this.

But still, I don't move.

What if Alex and Julie were to turn up right now, telling me that I don't have to do this and everything is fine? That we're still friends and I have everything I need right here, above ground?

I try to picture it but can't. Somehow it seems even less likely than Wonderland, Oz and Narnia combined.

No. I *do* have to do this.

Nodding once to myself, I take a deep breath, click on my head torch, and slip into the belly of Paris.

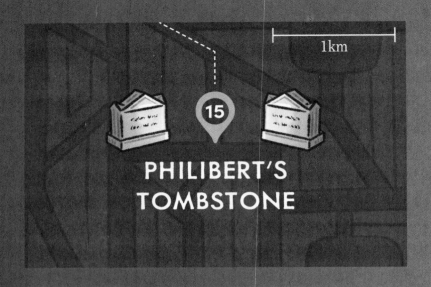

PHILIBERT'S TOMBSTONE

I find myself in a tunnel with a low ceiling. A damp smell greets me. I think about the 'champignons de Paris', the button mushrooms that were once grown down here. I read that by 1880 more than 300 mushroom farmers worked underground to produce more than 900,000 kilograms of mushrooms every year. But when the Métro was built in the late 19th century, it was the end of the underground mushroom farms. Today there are only five champignonniers left in the Paris area. And none of them are in the underground anymore.

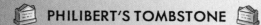

Maybe I'll revive underground mushroom farming when I grow up. I could be a cataphile *and* make money.

The tunnel hugs me. Some people might find it claustrophobic, but I like it. It makes me feel the limits of my own body, just like when I am wearing the vest or rubbing against the wall.

I walk in a crouch through the tunnel. The beam of my head torch dances across the limestone walls. Above me, the noise of the street is muffled; bus brakes, car horns, sirens – they can't reach me. Even the smell is bearable. Just dampness and mould. No wonder the mushrooms thrived down here.

Water splashes around my feet. I know exactly where I am; Claudine's map is all laid out in my mind. I'm heading right towards Philibert Aspairt's tombstone. That's where I'll meet some cataphiles, for sure. And if there are any clues to the location of the secret wine cellar, I'm sure I'll find them there.

After a few metres, the tunnel becomes larger and I can walk upright. My rucksack is no longer scraping against the ceiling. On the wall, a street sign tells me that I'm below *Boulevard Saint-Michel*. Twenty metres above me, people are eating their Dame Blanche at *Brasserie Splendid*, marvelling at the Métro wall map.

I take a left turn. There it is. An array of tea lights, battery-operated and real, illuminate an inscription on a simple rectangular tombstone. There are no cataphiles in sight, despite one live, flickering flame. How long does a tea light burn for? Two hours? Three? They must have been here recently. Someone has left a bunch of pink teddy bears as a tribute.

IN MEMORY OF
PHILIBERT ASPAIRT,
LOST IN THIS EXCAVATION
ON 3 NOVEMBER 1793;
FOUND ELEVEN YEARS LATER
AND BURIED AT THE SAME
PLACE ON 30 APRIL 1804.

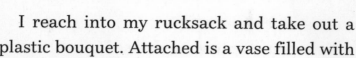

I reach into my rucksack and take out a plastic bouquet. Attached is a vase filled with fake plastic water.

As I place the vase next to the teddy bears, the tiny hairs on my arm stand up. This is a big moment. I'm honouring the patron saint of cataphiles, the community I hope to join.

The vase doesn't look as dignified as I'd hoped. But this is the underground, and you've got to work with what you've got. Philibert would understand.

I close my eyes. There is so much I want to tell him. That I came down here because the world above doesn't want me. That I'm looking for the bottle of chartreuse just like he was. If only he could give me an idea of where I should start looking.

Then someone calls my name.

'Hugo!'

I turn around. It can't be …

'Spy, where are you?'

It is. It's Alex and Julie! They're here! Just as I imagined earlier. Are they going to tell me we're still friends too?

Julie comes into view, dressed in wellington boots and a hooded coat. Alex follows, wearing the same trainers, tracksuit and light rain jacket he's been wearing all week. Not the ideal underground attire. They each carry a torch.

'There you are!' says Julie. She actually sounds happy to see me. It's almost as though my daydream has become reality. Then Alex walks up to me and I know that it hasn't. He grabs me angrily by my shoulder straps.

'Are you out of your mind?' he shouts. 'Mum meant to report that hole ages ago, and if she finds out I told *anyone* about it I will be in *big* trouble! We're leaving. *Now.*' He tries to pull me back the way we've come, but I don't budge.

'What's Julie doing here?' I ask.

'I was at Alex's for the science project,' Julie explains. 'I wanted to see the entrance to the catacombs he was talking about.'

'And then,' Alex fumes, 'we saw Madame Ginette practically patrolling the area. Apparently a *friend* of mine was poking around

the basement on Sunday and she thought he might be back!'

'We said it was just us this time,' Julie says. 'But then we found the gate off its hinges—'

'And I just *knew* it was you, Spy!'

'But he was too afraid to follow you down here himself.'

'I wasn't afraid!'

'You certainly didn't look like you were ready to do this alone. And you were happy to wait while I went all the way home to grab my wellies.'

Julie says this like she lives far away, but her house is almost as close to Alex's as mine is.

'You said you needed them!' Alex defends himself. 'And I knew we'd find him quicker together. I'm never afraid. Understand?' He pulls up his jumper to reveal a small tattoo on his forearm. He shoves it under my nose. 'You know what this is?'

'A necktie?' I guess.

'It's a katana sword, dumbo! A Samurai symbol for courage and bravery. If you know what those words even mean.'

'They mean the same thing,' I point out. 'They're synonyms.'

'Is that real?' Julie asks.

'Do I look like someone who would wear a fake tattoo?' Alex asks.

Yes, I think. But I remember what happened with Enzo when I was honest with him, so I don't say this out loud. Even though I'm pretty sure that tattooing kids is illegal.

'Now let's move it, Spy,' Alex orders.

'Impossible,' I say. 'I'm looking for a secret wine cellar. Nobody has been able to find it so far. But I will. And I won't leave until I have.'

'What's so important about a wine cellar?' Julie asks. For the first time in a long time, she sounds genuinely interested.

'It's a long story. You two should leave. I'll be fine.'

'Yeah, tell that to my mum,' Alex says. 'You're coming with us, Spy.'

'No.'

I don't move.

Alex grabs my jacket and tries to pull me with him again.

'Let go of me!' I yell, pushing him away. 'I'm not leaving, whatever you do!' The maps are in my head. I'm the leader of this expedition, even if he's the one with the tattoo (which I still think is fake). I don't need Samurai symbols, anyway. I have my photographic memory; and it's here in the underground that it'll rise to the surface – like my favourite apple beignets in Mum's deep fryer.

Alex finally lets go. Julie tilts her head at me and I scan her expression. Could she be surprised? I suppose I'm not normally this stubborn.

'Scorpion!' Alex suddenly yells, surprising all of us. As I turn around, Julie grabs my shoulders and hides behind my back. Alex is pointing at the limestone wall.

'Where?' I take a closer look. My head torch spotlights a spider, sitting on the wall above a graffitied zombie skull.

'That's just a spider, Alex. Totally harmless.'

'Shut up!' he hisses. 'I know what it is. I was just trying to scare you.'

Julie laughs and lets go of my shoulders.

'Spiders and scorpions both belong to the arachnid family, so it's a totally understandable mistake to make, Alex. My dad's afraid of spiders too,' I say. 'He calls Mum every time he finds one in the bathroom.'

Alex pushes me against the wall. 'I am *not* afraid, Spy. I don't even know what that word means. Are we clear on that? Remember the katana sword?'

I nod. *The fake one,* I think.

'I have a black belt in kung fu. I can break a piece of concrete with my bare feet. I've fought the Green Devil. Does that sound like I'm afraid?'

'It sounds like you're making stuff up,' I tell him, his lies now too outrageous for me to resist correcting them. 'The Green Devil is an urban legend. A subterranean urban legend, to be precise. And concrete doesn't break that easily.'

'You don't believe me?'

Alex lets go of me and stands before a man-made pillar: rough pieces of stone stacked one on top of the other, tapering in size. He bounces on his toes, his hands in front of his face, his elbows close to his body like a boxer. He shoots threatening looks at the pillar.

'You shouldn't touch that,' I say. 'It's limestone. It's much softer than concrete. And that pillar supports the ceiling.'

Alex doesn't listen. He kicks the pillar.

Nothing happens.

'Hi-yaa!' Another kick, faster and stronger. I hear a faint sound coming from the pillar. Alex pulls a face. That must have hurt.

'Stop it!' Julie tells him.

But Alex doesn't stop. His third kick is the strongest one, sending a ripple up the pillar. It shakes from left to right, like something in one of those earthquake films, announcing inevitable disaster. The shaking is followed by a loud crack, and then–

BOOM!

LOST

Alex jumps to the side. I shove Julie out of the way, sending us both to the floor. The pillar collapses like a set of building blocks. Part of the ceiling crashes down with it. A cloud of dust rises up and envelops us. The air is dry and powdery. I can taste the limestone in my mouth, like chewing chalk. I cough.

'Are you out of your mind?' Julie yells at Alex. 'You could have killed us!'

'Sorry. I had no idea it was that unstable,' Alex mumbles, still shocked by what just happened.

'Didn't you hear what Hugo said?'

I reach out my hand to help Julie get up again.

'Thanks.' She winces and rubs her left elbow. 'Ow. Can we go back now?'

But as the dust settles, we see that this isn't an option. Stones litter the ground where we just stood. Our route to the basement is blocked.

'It looks like the only way is forward,' I say.

Julie buries her face in her hands.

'You mean we're trapped?' Alex asks, sounding strange.

'We're not trapped. We just need to find another way out.'

Alex wipes his forehead with a shaking hand. 'Good.'

'Hey, are you OK?' Julie asks.

'You're breathing really fast,' I point out.

'Do you … think … there's enough?' he gasps out.

'Enough what?' Julie asks

'Oxy … gen.'

'Oxygen?' Julie looks as if the thought hadn't occurred to her. Both of them look panicked now as they turn to me.

'Of course there is,' I say. 'And don't worry. The underground is like a huge maze, but I know my way around.'

My words don't seem to be helping. If anything, Alex's breathing is getting worse.

I dig in my rucksack and take one of my sandwiches out of its brown paper bag. 'Here, breathe into the bag for ten breaths, it will help you calm down.' Mathilde showed me the trick a while ago. It helps you put lost carbon dioxide back into your bloodstream, which balances the oxygen flow in your body and stops you hyperventilating.

Alex does what I say. Slowly, his face relaxes. His brows unfurrow and the panic in his eyes melts away. He hands me the bag without a word.

'Already feeling better, right?' I enjoy being in charge. 'Here, wear these!' I throw the spare pair of hip waders to Alex, since Julie's has her boots.

He holds them up in front of him, where they resemble waxy dungarees with socks attached.

He wrinkles his nose. 'They're ridiculous.'

'You'll get wet without them. And cold.'

He puts them on.

'My phone!' Julie says suddenly. 'Why didn't I think of that before? We can call for help!' She reaches into her pocket and takes her smartphone out.

'The underground is too deep for phone coverage.' I hate to be the bearer of bad news.

'Give it to me,' Alex snaps. He grabs the phone from Julie's hands.

'Hey!' Julie protests. Alex jabs the screen only to discover that I'm right. Again. He really should just listen to me.

'Crap,' he mutters.

'I told you.'

'So how do we get out of here?' Julie asks.

'If the underground really is a maze, it'll be easy. There's a logic to mazes,' Alex declares.

Julie frowns. 'How do you know? You're terrible at maths ...'

'But amazing at *Labyrinth City*. I beat my cousin every time.'

I have more bad news: there is no logic to the underground. 'I said the underground is *like* a maze. It's not an actual maze. Being good at a video game won't help you.'

Alex's face drops.

Julie puts her hands on her hips. 'Forget games. My coach said that I have a really good sense of direction. When we got lost in Barcelona last year during the championships, I guided the entire swimming team back to our hotel. Follow me!'

Before I can point out that the underground is nothing like Barcelona, Julie takes the lead. She marches off down the tunnel, and Alex and I have no choice but to follow her. After a few minutes, I barely make out an inscription in the stone wall: '*Rue de l'Odéon*'. We turn left, then right. A gallery, then another tunnel. And there it is again: '*Rue de l'Odéon*'.

We're going in a circle! Should I say something? I don't want to upset Julie like I did Enzo. But it turns out that I don't need to. Two minutes later, we're back where we started.

'Great sense of direction,' Alex snorts, kicking a piece of rubble from the collapsed pillar.

'At least I tried! You haven't gotten us anywhere with your video game logic.'

'At least I didn't waste our time!'

I hold up a hand like I'm in class waving for the teacher's attention. 'Guys? I told you, I know my way around. I can get you out of here.'

I try to sound convincing while I review the route to the next exit where I can send Alex and Julie out. The truth is, I'm confused. According to Claudine's map, there should be a tunnel to our right, but there isn't. Instead, there is one to our left, which we take. This part of the underground is wetter. After a couple of minutes of walking, the puddles reach our ankles.

I turn to Alex. 'Good thing I insisted on the hip waders.'

Alex doesn't respond.

As we splosh through the flooded tunnels, Julie is right behind me, followed by Alex.

His breathing is still heavy and strained. We march for minutes without talking. Water runs down the walls in trickles. Where are we? I go through the maps in my head, trying to make sense of this maze. All I need is a point of reference, but there are none. I rub against the drier walls to calm myself. The tunnels are so tight that Alex and Julie don't notice.

What if the belly of Paris were a living organism? I think, trying to keep my anxiety at bay. 'You need to keep your mind busy,' Mathilde always says. 'That way it won't have time to panic.' So I imagine that Julie, Alex and I are like gut bacteria, moving through the underground's intestines. It makes me smile.

'Is this tunnel getting larger at some point?' Alex says. He's the tallest of us. He has to hunch to keep his head from touching the ceiling.

'Actually, this is still fairly large. Wait until we have to climb through a chatière,' I say. 'It'll be even smaller then.'

At the mention of the cat flap, Alex's breathing gets faster and louder again. He sounds like a steam engine. Could he be claustrophobic?

'Don't worry,' I quickly add. 'I'll make sure to avoid the chatières.'

My thoughts return to the map. The IGC has been working relentlessly to fortify the underground. There are no more large collapses like the one in 1961, when a giant sinkhole swallowed a neighbourhood in the southern part of the city and killed twenty-one people. But Claudine told me that small collapses like the one we just experienced happen all the time. Which means that the structure of the underground changes all the time. Just like a living organism changes through cell division, the underground changes through collapsing. I like that idea … except it also means that Claudine's map is not completely up to date. She's in charge of recording the changes and nobody has reported this change yet. It will be my duty to do it, once we're back home. But right now, we're lost.

I bring us to a standstill, trying to find my bearings.

'How far?' Alex demands, interrupting my thoughts.

'You don't know where we are, do you?' Julie asks.

'Right now, no,' I say, trying not to panic. 'But things can change at any moment.'

'Some map nerd,' Alex snorts. 'I need to be back tonight for Mum's lasagne. 7 p.m. That's all I'm saying.'

'Things can change at any moment,' I repeat.

'You already said that,' Julie points out.

'I need to put my thoughts back in order. Repeating stuff helps me do that.'

Julie groans. 'We're never getting out of here.'

'Yes, you are,' I say. 'I'm doing my best.' There's a system to the underground. It's not random tunnels. I just need to find a clue. Then I'll know where we are – and how to get out.

Out of nowhere, Alex grabs my jacket. His face is so close I can see the tiny sweat pearls on his upper lip.

'Do better!' he growls. 'You said you knew about this place!'

'I do!'

Now I'm angry. I may not know how to swim like Julie, or joke like Alex – but if there's one thing I *do* know it's the underground.

'I know all the monuments that were built using the limestone that came from these quarries! *Notre Dame*. The *Louvre*. The *Place de la Concorde*. The *Invalides*.'

'Fat lot of good that is!' Alex shouts back.

'I know the name of the guy who drew the first maps of the underground, more than 300 years ago!'

'I don't care what happened 300 years ago! I wanna get out of here *now*!'

'It was Charles-Axel Guillaumot!' I continue, a rising tide of panic and anger pushing the words out of me as I try to take back control. 'Because people had dug up so much limestone to build all those churches and monuments, there were sinkholes all over Paris. The city was collapsing. So Guillaumot built these underground walls along the same borders as the buildings above ground. And on each wall, he wrote a code. As soon as I find one of those codes, I'll know exactly where we are.'

'Well hurry up!'

'We're only in this situation because of *you*! *You* kicked that pillar.'

'Because you said I was afraid of spiders! I'm not afraid of anything.'

'Then why scream? Screaming means you're afraid.'

'STOP IT!' Julie shouts. She's been silent while Alex and I argue. 'If we want to get out of here, we'd better work as a team. Even if we don't like each other.'

Even if we don't like each other. A lump forms in my throat.

We march on in silence.

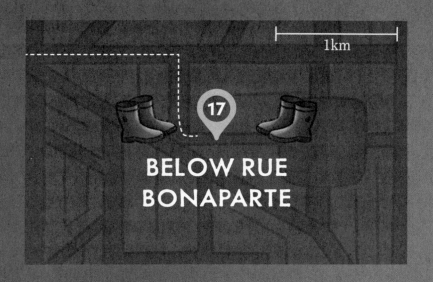

BELOW RUE BONAPARTE

As we walk, I go over the maps in my head. My eyes scan the walls for a number, a code, a clue – anything that will tell me where we are. And then I see it. A code engraved in the limestone: '4G1786'. I've seen pictures of these in books, but to see it in person gives me goosebumps. It's amazing how something written more than 300 years ago is still helping us today. Guillaumot invented the Google Maps of the 1800s.

'There. 4G1786. That number means this is the fourth wall built by Guillaumot in 1786. Right now, we're below *Rue Bonaparte*.'

'Wow. How do you know all of that?' Julie asks.

I like the way she says 'wow'.

'I remember everything I read. Mum says I'm like Superman, but no one knows if Superman has a super memory. We know he can hear sounds from far away, so in that sense we're a bit alike. The difference is that his ears are not like open microphones. He can screen out sounds and focus only on things that matter. That is precisely what my brain *can't* do.'

Superman can also hear sounds on other planets, which I can't – and that's totally fine with me. It's challenging enough dealing with sounds on Earth. What if I had to deal with sounds of the entire solar system, or worse, the entire galaxy?

'You're a weirdo,' Alex mutters.

I ignore his comment. Fuelled by Julie's admiration, I continue. 'When I see something, my brain takes a picture of it. That's how I remember stuff. I like patterns. Like maps or train schedules. I'm good at identifying and remembering patterns.'

'I wish I had that too,' Julie says. 'It would make studying *so* much easier! I could just look at a textbook and …' she clicks her fingers '… it would be in my head like that.'

I smile at her. Julie studies a lot. If she's not in the swimming pool, I see her at the school library.

This is the first normal conversation we've had in a long time. I want it to continue. I could choose not to tell her about the exit that's really close. But that wouldn't be fair.

'OK, listen,' I say. 'Before we go any further, two things: first, there's an exit in approximately two kilometres where you can leave the underground; second, I need to tell you about the rules of this place.'

'What do you mean, "rules"? I thought this was the Wild West? Anarchy and everything?'

Alex loves to talk about anarchy, although I'm pretty sure he doesn't know what it means. One of the skater kids he hangs out with has a T-shirt that says 'Anarchy!' That's where he saw it, I'm sure.

'Anarchy is a state of disorder that happens when there's no authority. Like that time when there was no teacher in the playground and you emptied a carton of milk over my head.' I probably should have chosen another example, but that's the one I care most about. I still want to know why he did it.

'Stop giving me lessons, Spy. I know what it means. What are these rules, then?'

'There is no anarchy in the underground because of the cataphiles. They make the rules,' I say. 'Rule number one: Respect the past of the catacombs. Don't destroy anything, and if you create, do so with care. Rule number two: Whatever you bring in you take out with you. Respect the environment, just like you would do above ground. Rule number three: Share everything you have with others. Rule number four: Help others when necessary.'

Alex cuts me off. 'So why is there nobody here to help us?'

'We don't need help, Alex. I'll get you two out. And finally, rule number five: No buying and no selling. All good?' I ask.

Alex and Julie nod.

'Then let's move on.'

Alex is puffing at the back. The fabric of my hip waders makes a funny sound, like a rubber duck being squeezed. Some sections of the tunnels we pass through are as dry as desert sand, then a few metres on we find ourselves knee-deep in clay-coloured water.

'My feet are getting wet!' Julie shrieks. Her wellingtons aren't tall enough to keep the water out.

I swivel my rucksack round and crouch. 'Piggyback?'

After a brief moment of thought, she climbs on. 'Thanks.'

'Hold tight.'

We continue sploshing through the water loudly, sending waves against the walls.

'Stop!' Alex says suddenly. I turn to find him doubled over like he's catching his breath.

'Come on,' I grunt, adjusting my arms under Julie's legs. She's getting heavy.

When Alex doesn't move – or even tell me to shut up – I realise he's looking at something. Our splashing has stopped but the surface of the water is still moving. Only now it's vibrating. A rumbling sound follows.

'Earthquake!' Alex yells. His face is sweating like the walls and his cheeks are red and blotchy. He looks like he did last Tuesday when he failed the maths test.

But there are no earthquakes in Paris.

'What is this, Hugo?' Julie yells right by my ear.

Another collapse? I think. I look around, expecting rocks to come crashing down on our heads at any moment. But nothing happens. The noise disappears. It's silent now, except for the ripples of water running down the walls of the tunnel.

Of course. It wasn't an earthquake or a collapse.

'It's the Métro!' I cry. 'We must be right underneath it. We're probably around twenty-five metres deep, and the Métro is at twenty.'

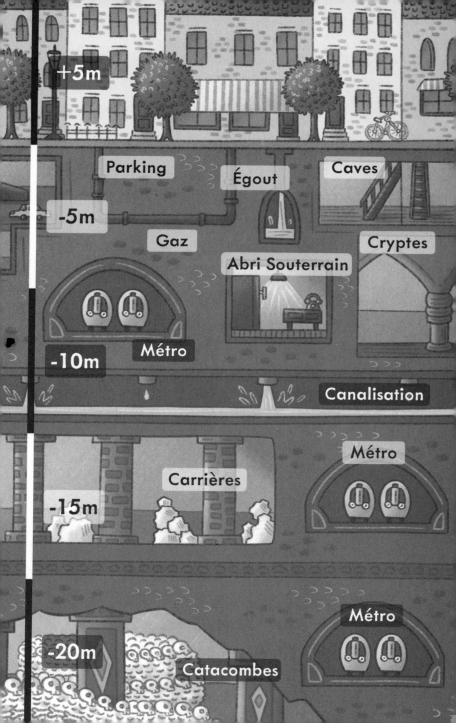

I'm smiling with relief, laughing at my own mistake. I think I see a similar expression on Alex's face too. I haven't seen him smile like that for a long time. At school he's too busy being cool to laugh at himself anymore.

'This place is too crazy for me,' Julie sighs, and her breath stirs my hair. 'I need to get out of here.'

'I'm on it,' I say.

'Spy, turn off your head torch. Every time I look at you, you're blinding me,' Alex says.

'OK. But you need to keep your torches on. Otherwise we won't see a thing.'

'Duh.'

After a few minutes, the underground changes again. The water gradually disappears. Julie slides off my back.

'Thanks for the ride.' She smiles at me.

'You're welcome.' For a moment, it feels like we're all friends again. But then another sound interrupts us, and I have to cover my ears. Still, it blasts through my brain like Mum's food mixer times ten. My heart races.

The source of the noise is close. *Very close.* It's coming from behind a wall, just a couple of metres from where we stand.

A wall with a ragged black hole in it.

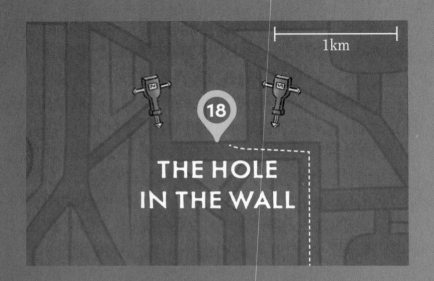

THE HOLE
IN THE WALL

The noise stops as abruptly as it started. I take my hands off my ears and stare at the hole. It's fresh, the limestone around the edges paler than the rest of the wall.

'There's someone there! We're saved!' Alex cheers, setting off towards it.

'Shhh! Wait!' I grab his arm and hold him back. 'Something doesn't feel right.' I move Alex's arm to train his torch away from the hole. 'Let me check it out first.'

I creep up to the hole and crouch to peer through. My mouth falls open. I'm looking right into a wine cellar. Not dark and dank like a cave, but softly lit and mysterious.

In the soft light I can see two men standing in front of an iron gate that divides the cellar in two. One of the men holds a cordless jackhammer. He's tall and thin, and he moves his head like a bird: nervous, quick, alert. As he looks around, I see that he's wearing a black mask with two holes for eyes.

Alex pushes me aside to see what I'm gaping at.

'It's Darth Vader!' he whispers.

'I know! They sell that mask in shops for €3.99. Lightsaber not included.'

Julie pushes Alex aside to have a look herself

'The other one's wearing the same mask! Darth Vader times two!'

'Shhhh,' I say. 'They mustn't see us.'

From outside the hole, we listen.

'It's useless,' Vader One says – the tall one. 'The bars go too far into the stone.'

'Try again,' says Vader Two. He looks like the exact opposite of Vader One: short and compact.

The return sound of the jackhammer sends shockwaves through my body. I clamp my hands over my ears but it still feels as though my head is about to explode. I breathe out in relief when the sound stops again. Vader One grunts behind his mask, throws the jackhammer to the floor and stamps his feet. I can't see his face, but I can tell he's angry.

'We need to get behind that gate! That's where the rest of our bottles are.'

What does he mean by 'our bottles'?

'Wanna drill the lock directly?' Vader Two asks.

'No, there's too much vibration – I might destroy it without opening it and then we'll really be in trouble.'

Vader One holds out his hand. 'Give me your Swiss army knife.' Vader Two starts digging in his pockets. 'It's been a while,' Vader One continues, 'but I can try to pick the lock.'

Vader Two freezes suddenly, with his hands still deep in his pockets. 'Ooooooor,' he says slowly, pulling something out of the right one, 'you could use this?' A key dangles from a silver chain. Vader One stares at it for a long moment.

'How did *that* end up in your pocket?'

'I swiped it from Noiseau.' Vader Two laughs. 'Seemed like it might come in handy.'

'Oh, you think?' Vader One's sarcasm is clear. 'And you decided not to mention it until now? What kind of thief are you?'

Vader Two no longer sounds triumphant. 'A forgetful one?'

'Forgetful and stupid!'

Vader One snatches the key and reaches through the bars to put it in the lock on the other side. There's a soft click. The ease with which the gate springs open only seems to make him angrier.

'I can't believe you let me wrestle with that jackhammer when you had the damn key in your pocket all along!'

'Sorry, boss.' Vader Two mutters. 'It won't happen again.'

'You're right about that. Get in there.'

Vader One shoves Vader Two into the second

part of the cellar. It's smaller than the other, with only one wine rack. Vader One begins to take the bottles and hand them to Vader Two. Vader Two then wraps them in bubble wrap before carefully placing them in a black bag on the floor. Once that bag is full, they move on to another. Then another.

My heart is pounding like the jackhammer. This could be the secret wine cellar Claudine told me about! The cellar that contains the bottle of chartreuse Philibert tried to steal more than 300 years ago!

The Vaders zip their bags, swinging one onto each of their backs and taking one in each of their hands.

'They're leaving! Hide!' I drag Alex and Julie behind a large pillar opposite the wall. 'Turn off your torches!' Alex does as I say quickly, but I have to nudge Julie before she turns off hers. I can't see either of them in the sudden darkness, only hear someone's – Alex's? – strained breathing. I peek around the pillar. Seconds later the Vaders appear through the hole. They hover for a moment. Only then, as they switch them on, do I realise that they've been wearing head torches over their Darth Vader masks the whole time. It may be an even worse look than my vest.

I wait until they disappear down a tunnel and we can't hear their footsteps anymore. Then Julie switches on her torch and I jump out from behind the pillar, heading straight for the hole in the wall. Alex follows me. Julie doesn't.

'Come on, what are you waiting for?' I whisper, although there's no need to anymore. The Vaders are long gone now, and I wonder where to.

'That's someone's wine cellar. We can't just go inside,' Julie says. I touch the hole. Small pieces of soft limestone fall to the floor, like crumbs from shortbread.

Julie is right. This is private property. Entering it would be against the law. But then so is exploring the underground. And what if this really is the wine cellar that Claudine talked about? I've come too far to turn back now.

'Come on,' I insist. 'There's nobody here. Let's just have a look!'

'OK,' Julie mutters. 'Just a look.'

We slip into the cellar through the hole, one after the other. I go first. I expect the air to be damp, like the rest of the underground, but it's surprisingly fresh and cool. I spot a ventilation system on the wall. Mould can damage a wine cellar and disturb the wine's aging process, Dad once told me. Dad – who knows almost as much about wine as he does about champagne – says that some people pay a fortune for it, but then they don't store it the right way and it goes bad. Clearly the owner of this wine knows what they're doing.

The walls of this part of the cellar are punctuated with arch-shaped niches, all framing wine bottles. The bottle necks are wrapped in red, black, yellow and golden foil. In the centre stands a table. Someone has put silver candleholders on it, and the melted wax makes me think that a dinner party was held here not long ago. Old-fashioned wall lamps are the source of the soft light I noticed earlier.

I walk over to the iron gate, where the floor is a mess of rubble, and push the gate open. The thieves have left the key swinging in the lock, and I'm reminded of Philibert's key rusting on his belt.

Alex and Julie follow me into the smaller part of the cellar. The bottles here are dustier than the ones in the first part. One has a layer so thick that small clouds form when I take it out of the rack. Alex coughs.

'Careful!' Julie whispers. 'Don't drop it! It looks super old.'

I wipe the bottle, revealing handblown, dark-green glass. The bottle is capped with a seal of thick yellow wax. There's no label, only the initials P.A. scratched into the glass in shaky writing. Followed by the year 1793.

'I was just thinking about him ...' I mumble, hardly believing it.

'Who?'

'Philibert.'

'Philibert? You mean the guy from the tombstone?' Alex asks.

I nod. 'He was the doorkeeper to the *Val-de-Grâce* military hospital who got lost in 1793 trying to steal this bottle from an underground cellar. His skeleton wasn't found until eleven years later.'

'Holy cow,' Alex mumbles. No jokes, no sneers – he sounds genuinely amazed.

'A bottle as old as that must be worth a lot,' Julie says.

'Then how come the thieves left it here?'

Alex has a point. I look at the rest of the dusty bottles.

'They didn't just leave the chartreuse,' I point out. 'This rack is still half full.' I turn to look back through the bars at the racks on the other side. 'So are the others.'

'That means they'll be back for more,' Julie says. 'And they won't be happy to find us here.'

Just then, I detect a strong smell. Like garlic, but not the kind Mum uses in her cooking. This smells like someone tried to chemically engineer the clove in a lab. I turn around and see a dark figure. I want to run. But all I manage is to quickly put the bottle back, then use the rack to hold myself up as my legs start shaking.

IN TROUBLE

'Vaders!' Alex yells – and unlike with the scorpion and the earthquake, this time he's right. Julie screams.

'Calm down,' Vader Two tells us. 'We're just after the wine.'

'What the hell are you guys doing down here?' Vader One asks. I can't see his face because of the mask and I'm wondering what his expression could be. Surprise? Annoyance?

'We just came down to get him,' Alex replies, pointing at me. It's the truth, but I find myself shaking my head. Vader One looks at Alex's finger.

'What are you, a snitch?' he steps closer and Alex steps back. 'You know what they did to snitches in the Middle Ages?' He reaches into his pocket. Does he have a knife? A gun? 'They hanged and chopped them into little pieces.'

Far from breathing quickly, now I'm not sure Alex is breathing at all. Julie is wide-eyed. For a moment nobody moves. Then Vader Two laughs.

'He's just joking, guys! Trying to lighten the mood.'

I'm no expert at understanding jokes – but that definitely wasn't funny.

'We're not here to chop anyone up,' Vader One confirms. 'We just want to get these bottles out without any trouble. Do as you're told and nothing ... bad ... will ... happen.'

As he says these last words, Vader One points a spidery index finger at each of us. I've never seen an index finger that long before. His hand reminds me of the cover of THE GREEN DEVIL graphic novel, creeping out of the manhole. His other hand finally leaves his pocket and tosses something to Vader Two.

'I'll pack the rest. You tape them to the gate.'

'You can't do that!' Julie shouts. 'We're kids!'

Vader Two looks at the roll of duct tape. 'She's right. We should just let them go.'

'Let them go so they can alert the police? No, tape them up. Hands and mouth. Noiseau has a tasting tonight. He'll find them then, and we'll be long gone.'

Noiseau? As in *Chef* Noiseau? They said 'tasting' …

'He's having the Rotary Club down here tonight at eight for a "pre-opening" party,' Vader One says, replying to something I've missed. 'Not that they'll have much to drink.' He chuckles.

'Why's that?' Vader Two asks.

'… Because we stole his best wine, Einstein.'

'Oh, yeah. Right. Nice one, Louis.'

'Don't use my name in front of the kids!' Vader One hisses.

'Oops. Sorry. I forgot.'

'You've got a memory like a sieve. Speaking of which, don't forget the Romanée-Conti from 1945. That's the one he wants most.'

'Got it, boss.'

I pretend not to listen, but I'm taking notes in my head.

- Darth Vader One = Louis (the boss). Smells of garlic (synthetic).
- Darth Vader Two = (name unknown). Not very bright, but much friendlier than Louis. Bad memory. Also smells of garlic (synthetic).
- They seem to be working for someone else (potential Emperor Palpatine?)
- Which 'Noiseau' are they talking about?

Philippe Noiseau is the most famous chef in Paris. I know this because Mum took one of his super-expensive cooking classes. If anyone could afford this much wine it's him. Every year he hosts the Noiseau d'Or, a sort of Olympic Games for cooks held right here in Paris, during which the world's best chefs compete against each other. Only this year he had to cancel the event because of a rat infestation in his restaurant.

If I'm right, Louis must have access to Philippe Noiseau's kitchen to know that they are having a wine tasting tonight. And this wine cellar must be connected to Noiseau's restaurant, *L'Accord*. If he's the current owner of Philibert's bottle, could he be a cataphile as well?

Vader Two tapes our hands around the gate with difficulty, especially Julie's.

'Can you give me a hand, boss?' he grunts, as he struggles to wrestle her arms behind her back. 'She's strong.'

'She's just a *girl*, don't be so pathetic.'

Eventually, Julie's hands are secured and Vader Two moves on to taping our mouths.

'Ow! She bit me!'

'Give me that,' Vader One mutters as he strides over, snatching the roll from Vader Two's hands and finishing the job himself. 'That's better. Right, princess?'

Julie's eyes narrow above the band of black duct tape. Beneath it she makes angry grunting noises.

'No one's going to hear us down here anyway,' Alex protests, turning his head away when it's his turn.

Vader One slaps the tape into place '*I can hear you, snitch. And you're annoying me.*'

'I'll get back to the bottles, boss,' Vader Two says, moving away from us.

Please don't let them take the chartreuse, I think.

'You haven't said anything yet,' Vader One says, looming over me.

I open my mouth to change that, but nothing comes out. The black grill at the bottom of his mask is wet with his breath. His eyes are a cold, piercing blue. And I'm a small shadow in the centre of his plastic forehead.

I close my mouth and swallow hard.

'Introvert, eh?' He rips off a piece of duct tape and smacks it over my mouth. 'Good.'

Fear replaces any curiosity. This isn't a

mystery, it's a drama – maybe even a thriller. And what comes after a thriller? *A horror.*

The sticky duct tape pulls at my cheeks. The intense smell of plastic makes me dizzy, and seems to grow stronger as it warms to my skin. I want to rub against a wall. I want my vest. I swear I wouldn't care how it looked.

The thieves wrap each bottle in bubble wrap before slipping it into their bags. They proceed carefully, handling the bottles like treasure.

'What's this?' Vader Two asks. 'There's no label. Just some letters and a date.'

I hold my breath.

Vader One glances at the dusty green bottle. 'It's old. Just take it.'

And with that, the chartreuse disappears.

'OK,' Vader One says at last. 'That's everything that was on the list, right?'

'Right,' Vader Two agrees. He sneaks a piece of paper out of his leather jacket, glances at it and quickly stuffs it back without Vader One seeing. 'That's everything.'

'Good. Let's get out of here.'

Vader One puts the bottle of chartreuse into the rucksack. By now they've emptied almost the entire wine rack this side of the cellar.

'Don't forget to take some more random bottles too. We need to cover our tracks,' Vader One instructs him.

'Like this Spanish one?' Vader Two takes a bottle and holds it up.

'That's Italian, stupid. But yeah. Take a few more of those.'

Vader Two complies, grabbing the few bottles left on the rack. Vader One goes to the other side of the cellar and takes some there too.

'OK, we're good to go,' Vader One announces, high-fiving Vader Two. The sound echoes like a gunshot. Are they really going to leave us here? We haven't even seen their faces. We can't identify them. I come to life, grunting, trying to make this point. Alex and Julie violently throw themselves from one side to the other, but it's useless.

'Sorry, kids. We just need a little bit of a head start here. In three hours, you'll be free.

See that door?' Vader Two points to a brushed silver door in the right-hand wall on our side of the cellar. 'Behind that is a lift that leads to Philippe Noiseau's restaurant upstairs. His clients are too posh to enter through manholes.'

So I was right. They *were* talking about the Chef Noiseau.

'Can't you just shut up?' Vader One snaps. 'They don't need to know everything. Now let's move it. We have to get back to … you know where.'

What's their plan? I wonder, scanning the map in my head. They won't be able to escape the underground through a manhole with those bags. In disbelief we watch them close and lock the iron gate.

CLANG!

Then the Vaders disappear through the hole they've drilled on the other side of the cellar, taking their jackhammer with them.

Leaving us bound and locked behind iron bars twenty metres under Paris.

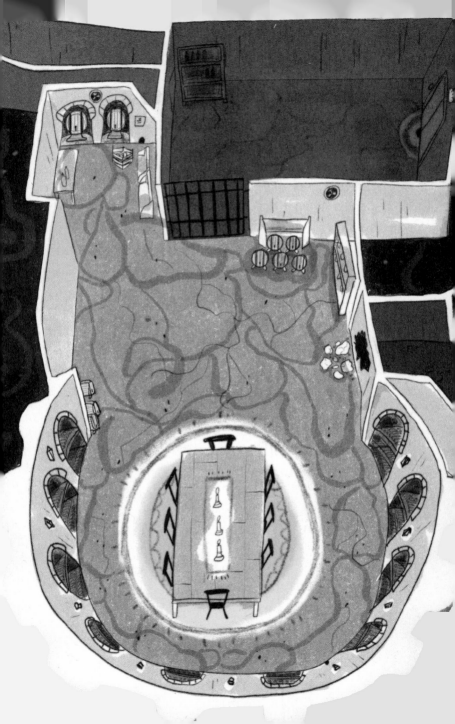

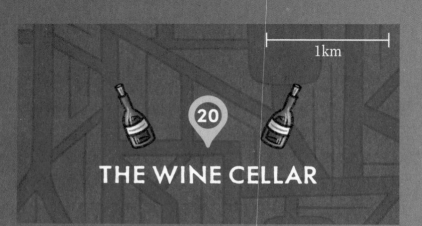

THE WINE CELLAR

The duct tape is wrapped tightly around my hands, cutting off my circulation. It feels like a million ants are crawling up my arms.

I glance at Julie. Her eyes are closed in concentration, her shoulders hunched up to her ears. With quick, jerking movements, she moves her hands up and down, sawing and pulling the tape against the bar behind her. The iron is slightly rough, I realise, feeling the bars behind my own back and trying to copy her. It's hard work. I'm tired and she's loose before I've even begun. With her hands free, Julie rips the duct tape off her mouth and spits in disgust.

'Swimming,' she explains as I stare at her, 'it

keeps your shoulders strong and flexible.' Then she rips the duct tape off my mouth and I yelp.

'Ow!'

'Thanks,' Alex gasps soon after me.

'Swimming taught me to never give up,' Julie continues. 'Never. Even if you're last in a race, you can still win.' She rattles the iron gate. Unlike the one to Alex's basement, it doesn't budge. We're not getting out of here without a key.

'Why did I follow you down here, Spy?' Alex sighs. 'Why?'

'Because you were afraid that your mum would find out that you bragged about the underground access in your basement?' I suggest. Did he already forget? It was only a couple of hours ago.

'Oh, shut up, Spy!'

I shake my head. Humans are confusing.

'We'd better find a way out of here,' Julie says. 'We have to stop those Vaders!'

I'm not sure if Julie is more bothered about the stolen bottles or being tied up and left here, but I don't care. I'm just happy that Julie wants to chase the wine thieves with me. I have to get the chartreuse back.

'Alex, you're with us, right?' Julie asks. 'Your kung fu training may come in handy.'

'I guess so, yeah.'

I'm sure that Alex would rather just leave as soon as possible and be home for his mum's 7 p.m. lasagne. But the way Julie asks her question doesn't leave him much choice – not after all his bragging about the katana sword tattoo and his supposed kung fu skills. If he backs out now, he'll lose all his credibility – but I can tell he wants to.

'Let's try the restaurant Wi-Fi!' Julie takes out her phone again and looks for local connections.

'Forget it. We're ten or fifteen metres below the restaurant,' I say. 'There's no way the Wi-Fi signal would make it through all that rock and stone.' The Vaders must have known that or they'd have checked us for phones.

'Then what?' Julie asks impatiently. 'Guys, we need a plan B. Come on. Think.'

'"His clients are too posh to enter through manholes ..."' I say.

'Come again?' Julie asks.

'The lift!'

As one we run to the door in the right-hand wall. There's only one button and I jab it hard. We wait. Alex presses his ear to the metal.

'I don't hear—'

The door slides open silently, revealing a small, elegant interior. There's a white floor bordered by a thin black square, and the name '*L'Accord*' in gold script in the centre. The panelled wood walls reveal two buttons at chest height. I jab the one with an upward arrow excitedly. We wait. I jab again. We wait some more.

'Nothing's happening,' Julie observes.

There's no emergency help button, only a smooth plate of glass above the up/down arrows that looks like a mirror.

'I think maybe you need a key card,' I say. 'We stayed at a hotel once and the button for our floor wouldn't even light up until we scanned the card.'

Alex kicks the wall with a growl.

'Good idea. Maybe sound will travel up the shaft and someone will hear it.' I hammer on the walls with both fists as I speak. Julie joins in, but between us we produce only a dull thumping sound.

'They're too thick,' Alex says

'We could go back to the cellar and dig a tunnel under the gate?' I offer.

'Dig?' he asks. 'With what?'

'The metal candlestick holders?'

'Yeah, good luck with that. They're on the other side of the cellar. And even if they weren't, it would take years.'

'Alex, all you do is criticise,' Julie says. 'You haven't said anything productive yet.' I appreciate her support, but I am afraid that Alex might be right. I remember a film where the hero dug a tunnel to escape from prison. It took him forever.

'I'm done with this.' Alex pushes me out of the lift. 'It's *your* fault we ended up here, so *you* find a way to get us out!'

Julie pulls him away from me. 'Stop it! We're in this together. What did I say about working as a team?'

'That we should do it even if we don't like each other?' I recall, with the same lump is my throat as before.

'Exactly,' Julie nods.

Even if now you hate my loud voice and the way I bounce up and down like a ball when I'm excited about a new idea, I think to myself. *Even if now you laugh at me for wearing sunglasses on a rainy day, or when I have to put on headphones to keep out noises you can't even hear.*

Even if now I embarrass you.

STILL THE
WINE CELLAR ...

With no other option, we try to dig under the gate. Limestone is a soft stone, but it's still stone. After fifteen minutes spent scrabbling around with our hands and a bottle opener Alex found, we haven't made a dent. Our hands are off-white with dust, and Julie's blue fingernails have turned grey. I'm reminded of therapy sessions with Mathilde when we chiselled elephant sculptures out of ytong, a lightweight cement. It was aimed at improving fine motor skills such as handwriting and knot-tying – but it was a lot more fun than this.

'Look!' Julie exclaims. 'That means we're going to be lucky!' She digs a rusted horseshoe out of the ground the Vaders turned up with their jackhammer. 'Finding a horseshoe in the underground – what are the odds, right? I wonder where it came from.'

'The odds are actually quite high,' I say 'In the old days, people used horses down here to haul stones. Maybe in a couple of centuries, someone will find our torches and wonder where they came from and what happened to their owners.'

The smile disappears from Julie's face. Too late I realise that this might not have been the best thing to say to her.

A rumbling noise makes me jerk. Julie takes my arm, clearly wondering the same thing: Is this another collapse? A Métro line passing above our heads?

'It's my stomach,' Alex mumbles. He sounds embarrassed.

I open my rucksack.

'Here, eat this. It's peanut butter.'

Alex hesitates for a second. Then he snatches the sandwich out of my hand as if he fears I might change my mind.

'Hanks,' he says with his mouth full.

'You're welcome.'

'Can I have one too, please?' Julie asks. 'I mean, if you have any left.'

'I have. We can share it.' I packed for a solo mission. Now there are three of us. I take the other sandwich out and give her half. It isn't much. 'I have protein bars as well,' I reassure her. 'Fruit and nut ones for slow-release energy.'

'Thank you.' When Julie takes the sandwich, she squeezes my hand. Her grip is strong, but it feels great. It feels like old times, when Pangea was whole.

I check my watch. It's 3.30 p.m. Another four and a half hours until the wine tasting. And what if Vader One got the week wrong? What if the wine tasting is next week and not today?

'Sooner or later, someone will come looking for us,' I say, trying to be more reassuring this time. 'I know Alex won't have told his mum we were coming down here, but I bet Julie told her parents. Right, Julie?'

'No.'

'Really?' My voice is sharp enough to make her look at me. 'I'm sorry, I just ... I thought you of all people–'

'What do you mean, "me of all people"?'

'You know, you're so perfect.'

Alex sniggers. Julie looks surprised. But how can she be? She's the school's best student. A swimming champion. Always perfectly dressed, with a perfectly symmetrical face and perfectly obedient hair. Even now, after traipsing through the underground, it refuses flyaways. It tucks neatly behind her ear as she looks at me and slowly tilts her head to the left. She does that a lot when she's trying to figure stuff out, I've noticed. The motion activates the right brain, the one that deals with emotions.

But all she says is, 'Trust me, Hugo, I am *not* perfect.'

'I bet you tell your parents everything, don't you, Spy?' Alex says.

'Not about this,' I say. 'I just wrote them a letter telling them that I'd left.'

Dark thoughts enter my mind. Years from now they'll find me. Or rather they'll find a pair of hip waders attached to my skeleton. Because that's all that'll be left, the synthetic rubber refusing to biodegrade. Somehow Philibert's story with the chartreuse and the keys still attached to his belt sounded way more mysterious. I don't want rubber and bone to be all that's left of me.

I reach into my rucksack, take out a piece of paper and start to write. By hand.

'What are you doing?' Julie asks.

'I want to leave a letter for my family,' I say, avoiding her gaze. 'Just in case someone doesn't find us in time.'

Alex laughs, but it sounds nervous. 'Don't be such a drama queen! Someone will find us. At some point Noiseau will have to get some wine from his cellar.'

'I have some more paper and a pen, if you want to do the same.'

'I'll take one,' Julie says.

'Alex?' I hold out a piece of paper.

He shakes his head and watches Julie and I write.

Dear Mum, Dad and Zoé,

I hope you'll never have to read this letter, because this was not supposed to end this way.

I came down here to look for a special bottle of chartreuse that's important to the cataphile community. Claudine at the Bibliothèque Historique told me it's somewhere underground, in a secret wine cellar. I wanted to find the cellar and return the chartreuse to her and the other cataphiles so that I could be one of them.

That was the plan, anyway. But we witnessed a robbery from Chef Noiseau's wine cellar (including the chartreuse). The thieves locked us in and... well, you can guess the rest.

If you find my skeleton like they found Philibert's, I want you to know that I love you all very much, and I'm sorry.

Hugo

P.S. All I can tell you about the wine thieves is that there were two of them. The one in charge was called Louis, but I think they were working for someone else. Both smelled of garlic, but not the kind Mum uses in her garlic bread. It was more of a chemical smell.

P.P.S. I'm really going to miss Mum's garlic bread...

P.P.P.S. Speaking of food — the other two skeletons are Alex and Julie's. They followed me down here.

P.P.P.P.S. By 'speaking of food', I don't mean that we ate each other. I mean that Alex missed his mum's lasagne. We may not be friends anymore, but we aren't cannibals either. ! · ·

By the time I finish adding postscripts, Alex is snoring. Julie has closed her eyes too. And I'm starting to feel panicky. Not enough to feel I need to stim yet, but enough to make me fixate on how panic feels a lot like excitement, only higher up – like the butterflies are in your chest instead of your stomach.

I remind myself that Alex is right. They *will* find us. This isn't the South Pole. We're only a lift ride from civilization.

I roll my letter up and slide it onto an empty groove in the wine rack, like a scroll in the lost Library of Alexandria. I think of Claudine, and of the South Pole again; of Robert Falcon Scott's failed mission to reach it first and return alive in 1912.

The chartreuse is like my South Pole. Will these be my last words before I fall asleep like Scott did?

I try to keep my eyes open, but my lids are heavy. I'm tired. From digging, from arguing and most of all from navigating an environment that's more dangerous than I thought. Writing by hand doesn't help. The focus required exhausts me. It's why I use a laptop at school.

I yawn despite myself, settling back against the cold stone wall next to Julie.

Random thoughts enter my mind: Mum in the kitchen. The banana tree in Julie's selfie at the *Jardin des Plantes*. Claudine's thick silver braid. And then I'm gone. Dreaming about the Green Devil cultivating mushrooms in the World War II bunker, Scott's frozen body and his last diary entry: *'It seems a pity, but I do not think I can write more ...'*

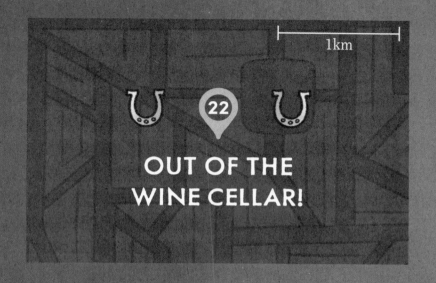

OUT OF THE WINE CELLAR!

I sleep for half an hour. The second I wake up I worry that Julie has seen the drool leaving a sticky snail's trail from the corner of my mouth. But she's still fast asleep. I sit up slowly, noticing that Alex is awake now too and putting something in his jacket.

I'm thirsty, but since I'm the only one who brought any water, we only have one bottle left for the three of us. And I already need a pee. I take an empty bottle out of my bag, eyeing the security cameras for a blind spot that might serve as a bathroom.

'What are you looking for?' Alex's voice makes me stop. There's no way I'm going to pee into a bottle in front of Alex. I'll have to wait.

'Ugh,' Julie grimaces, waking up and rubbing her eyes. 'I was hoping it was just a bad dream.'

'That we're trapped in a wine cellar fifteen metres underground?' I say. 'Afraid not.'

Alex refuses to be distracted.

'Spy, what are you hiding behind your back?' He gets up and comes closer.

'N-nothing,' I stutter. If he sees me holding the bottle, he'll know I was planning to pee in it. Then *Julie* will know.

Alex makes a grab for my arms and I veer into the wine rack. It rattles with the impact. The rack isn't fixed to the wall, I realise. It's on wheels.

'Wait,' I say softly, pushing Alex away from me. I've read enough mystery novels to know that moveable furniture usually hides a) a secret doorway, or b) a hidden treasure. Pushing the wine rack to the left, I pray for the former.

'Oh look, Spy discovered more wall,' Alex cheers sarcastically. 'Just in case we were bored with the rest – now we can stare at this bit.'

I touch the wall, ignoring him. It's limestone like the rest. What was I thinking? That it would open up and reveal a secret passage to freedom?

I start to roll the wine rack back into place, looking down so that Alex won't see my disappointment and guess the cause. There, right where my feet just were, is a plate in the floor. It's painted the same beige colour as the surrounding stone – like it's meant to go unnoticed. The paint is even rough and textured. There's a small button in the left corner.

'What is it?' Julie asks, joining me in a crouch to inspect it. I gently push the button, and all of a sudden the plate opens up, as if by magic. But I don't believe in magic. This is an automatic trapdoor.

Alex and Julie step back.

'Holy cow,' Alex mutters.

I look down the hole and see an iron ladder.

I feel like Houdini right now. Like one of those Las Vegas magicians who make elephants disappear on stage – only I've made something appear. *A way out.*

'You're a genius!' Julie shrieks, jumping up and down. 'We're free!'

'But who knows where it leads to?' Alex asks.

'We don't have much of a choice. Either we die of hunger or thirst right here in the cellar…'

'Not an option!' Julie says.

'… or we try this tunnel and see where it leads,' I conclude.

'OK, but you go first,' he says, eyeing the vanishing ladder. With nerves like that, Alex is the exact opposite of a samurai. He doesn't deserve a katana sword tattoo. Not even a fake one from the shop.

I turn on my head torch and lower myself into the hole, holding on to the iron rungs and climbing into the darkness. The dry roughness of the ladder gives me goosebumps. Or maybe it's fear of what could be lurking at the bottom. The underground seems less like the small intestine now and more like a mouth swallowing me whole. I hum a nervous tune, even though it means I have to breathe through my nose, letting in the sting of rusty metal.

After what feels like a long way but is in reality only a couple of metres, my feet find solid ground. I whip my head left and right to reveal only an empty tunnel. Then I look up and light the way as Julie and then Alex begin their descents. I count each rung. When Julie is on the fifth, Alex is on the first. Sixth, second. Seventh, third. Eighth, fourth. And so on until Julie has reached me, and I feel calm.

'Why would Noiseau put a trapdoor in there?' Julie asks. She dusts off her jacket and turns on her torch. 'Anybody could access the wine cellar from this side.'

At that very moment, we hear a soft whirring sound followed by a loud click, like a lock closing. The metal plate is back in its original position above our heads.

'It must be for Noiseau's private use,' I say. 'Maybe he's a member of the UX.'

We're in a different part of the underground now, at an even deeper level. It makes me think of Mum's layered cake that she always makes for my birthday. Which layer are we in exactly? I look for clues on the limestone walls – one of Guillaumot's numbers or a street sign – but I can't see any yet. At least the ceiling allows us to stand upright, and the air is dry.

'What's the UX?' Julie asks as we walk.

'It stands for Urban eXperiment, a group of underground explorers. Trapdoors are one of their many inventions to connect different parts of the underground.'

'Why?' Alex asks.

'To get to different places above and below Paris,' I say. 'They built a secret underground cinema a while ago, beneath the Eiffel Tower.'

Julie smiles, the way she always smiled when I told her one of my map facts. She's actually listening to me. She hasn't done that for a long time.

'Sounds like your kind of folk, Spy,' Alex says. 'Nerd central.'

Is this a compliment? It feels like one. The UX are cool. I read all about their crazy feats after Claudine told me about them. They never reveal their identities. They never talk about what they do – unless it becomes public because the press talks about it. Then they acknowledge it only to disappear again. 'Ne cherchez pas'. *Do not search.*

'It's said that they have access to every government building, every telecom tunnel. They have all the maps and all the keys,' I say. 'One time they staged a Shakespeare play at the World War II bunker and ...' I stop walking. I grab Julie by the shoulders. 'The bunker! That's where the wine thieves took the wine!'

'What?'

'I had a dream about it in the wine cellar. The Green Devil was cultivating mushrooms.'

'Are you sure you're OK?' Julie is frowning now.

I try to slow down. 'The World War II bunker is an old Nazi headquarters. It has direct access to the basement of the *Lycée Montaigne*, my sister's school. It would be a perfect hideaway for thieves! During the evenings, the school is probably empty. The Vaders could easily carry the bottles to the surface through the school's basement, without having to pass through a manhole with all their bags.'

I jump up and down, feeling this exciting flash of inspiration through my entire body.

'How do we get there? We need to find them before they leave!' Julie says.

And before they take the bottle of chartreuse with them!

'Wait. Why?' Alex asks Julie, alarmed.

'Alex, we witnessed a theft. These people are criminals! We have to catch them!'

'More like you want revenge for them saying you're just a girl.'

I hadn't thought of that, but Julie doesn't deny it. She folds her arms and shrugs. 'That too.'

Alex sighs. 'Whatever. So long as I'm home for seven.'

I look around. On my left is a blue enamel plaque set into the wall: '*Avenue Reille*'.

'This way!' I say, pointing down a tunnel to my right. I smile at Julie, unable to hide my excitement. My face hurts from it. Julie's own face is suddenly ashen.

'There … that – that thing …' she stutters, pointing at something behind me. I turn around, expecting to see a bat or another spider. My heart stops. This is no bat. No spider.

It's the Green Devil!

I look at him for a split second. He's bald. Two horns grow from each side of his green head. His hand grips a thick iron chain. I'd told myself he was only a legend, but the moment I look into the Green Devil's eyes a very real chill goes up my spine.

'Run!'

Alex and Julie don't need to be told twice. We sprint faster and faster into a tunnel, into darkness strobed by torchlight as my head bobs and Alex and Julie's arms pump. I try to keep my balance on the muddy, uneven terrain. At a junction, I take the left tunnel.

'This way!' I shout. Alex and Julie follow me.

I don't have time to analyse our route. All I can think about are those eyes. I've never been so afraid in my entire life. I keep thinking I hear the Green Devil's feet right behind us, his iron chain clanking.

'Speed up!' Julie yells, like she can hear it too. But we're already running as fast as we can, drawing level with each other when the tunnel is wide enough, filtering into single file when it isn't. One minute I'm in the lead. The next Julie. Then Alex. I'm gasping for breath, a sharp stitch developing in my side. Then I see the words '*Rue Saint-Jacques*' engraved in the stone ahead.

'Alex! Julie!' I gasp. 'There! The hole in the wall on your right! Go through it!'

There's a pause, then, 'It's too small!' Alex insists.

'Just get in there!' I shout, careening into his back.

'I can't!'

The mouth of the tunnel is barely as wide as our shoulders. On Claudine's map it said chatière. And a cat flap is exactly what this looks like. There's no way the Green Devil will be able to follow us.

'You can do it, Alex! I know you can!' I squeeze his shoulder. For a second, I feel like he's going to pull away. Then he nods tightly.

I turn around. The Green Devil must be on our heels. We have no time to lose.

'Julie, you go first. Alex in the middle. I'll follow. It's a short passageway. You'll be out in no time.' I don't tell them what's on the other side. I'm not sure they'd crawl through if they knew.

Alex still looks nervous.

'What if I get stuck?'

'This is meant to fit grown-ups,' I point out. 'If they don't get stuck, we won't.'

Julie takes Alex by the shoulders and looks him in the eyes. 'Take a deep breath. You can do this.' This must be the way her swimming teacher talks to her.

Alex gives Julie a nod. Sweat pearls on his forehead as we watch Julie diving into the hole.

I gently push Alex after her. Then it's my turn. The tunnel is tight, hugging my body like the vest. I think about a film Mathilde showed me about Temple Grandin, the scientist who invented a hug machine for people on the autism spectrum. People like me. This chatière works like a giant hug machine for me, but Alex is grunting like a piglet. Every couple of seconds, Julie shouts something motivational at him in order to keep him moving.

'It's a mind game!'

'You can do this!'

All that shouting may work for breaking swimming records, but I'm not sure it's a great technique to make Alex forget that he's crawling through a passageway as tight as a gas pipe. Distracting him with more fun stuff seems like a better idea. I feel like a worm right now, so I tell Alex about the day rainworms fell from the sky in Norway. The poor worms had been swept up by the wind and got caught by thermals – rising pockets of warm air – that carried them up into the sky.

'But eventually the rainworms fell back to Earth as worm rain! True story!' I chuckle. Alex doesn't seem to find this wordplay funny. 'You know, "rainworms" – "worm rain",' I explain. 'Hey, Alex, think how much easier this would be if you were a rainworm. The worm's skin makes this fluid to help it move through underground burrows and–'

'Be quiet, Spy! I need to concentrate,' Alex gasps.

Suddenly, a loud scream echoes through the tunnel. It's followed by a crunching, crackling sound, like someone's walking on broken porcelain.

Or broken bones.

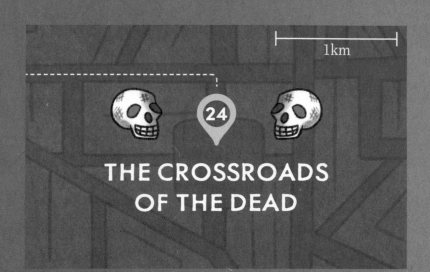

THE CROSSROADS OF THE DEAD

Alex and I pop out behind Julie, into a vast chamber where we can stand upright again. There are bones everywhere. Skulls. Pelvises. Shin bones. Thigh bones. They're not neatly piled or stacked the way they are in the official part of the catacombs – the ossuary that's open to the public every day of the week (except Mondays). This place is not a tourist attraction. It's a mess. An ocean of bones, littering the floor like withered white leaves.

'*Seriously?*' Alex exclaims.

'What is this place?' Julie shrieks. 'It looks

like a something out of a horror film!'

'This is the Crossroads of the Dead,' I say. 'It's an underground graveyard. Which means we're right under *Montparnasse* now. In the 18th century, the Paris cemeteries were overflowing, so they dumped the remains of six million people underground. Many of them had infectious diseases. The plague, cholera, gangrene–'

'Stop it!' Julie's face scrunches in disgust.

'I'm sorry I had to bring you here, but it was the only way to escape the – I mean, that creature,' I say.

Alex backs up against a wall and puts his head in his hands. He's still shaking.

'Speaking of which,' Julie says. 'Alex, was that the same creature you fought "*Mortal Kombat* style" the other day? The Green Devil?'

'I don't know *what* that was!' Alex yells, gripping fistfuls of his hair. 'I lied! I never fought the Green Devil!'

'Yeah, we kind of knew that,' I say. 'But the more important question is, is he even real?' He? She? It? What's the proper pronoun for a non-human, non-animal creature?

'What do you think?' Julie asks me. 'You're the expert on the underground.'

'I don't know,' I reply, savouring the compliment. Devils don't exist. But what about those toxic green eyes? And the horns? Could they have been fake?

'What I do know is that he scared us enough

to make us run for our lives,' I say. I might have broken a personal record in the process.

'Yeah. Straight into the chamber of death …' Julie looks around at the bones, shivering.

'I still can't believe I managed to wiggle through that tiny tunnel,' Alex says, sounding calmer. In fact, now he sounds in awe of his own courage. 'I can't even take a lift without sweating like crazy!'

Julie shakes off her unease to congratulate him. 'Well done, Alex. Great teamwork, guys.' She high fives us both.

My knees ache from crawling on stone, but I don't care. We're a team! A warm feeling fills me up from head to toe. Could it be that the continents are drifting back together again?

'Come on, we need to get to the World War II bunker quickly,' I say.

There's no choice but to step on the bones, which feels awful in more ways than one. The colours range from yellowish-grey to orange-brown, so different from the bright white bones of our biology class skeleton. I hear Julie apologising each time one cracks; Alex cursing each time they give way and he falls, which is often. Eventually, we just have to crawl again.

'This is so gross,' Julie whispers, using a femur to spread her weight more evenly.

'They're just bones. Nothing to be afraid of.' Alex grabs a skull and plants his torch inside it. 'BOO!'

'Stop it!' Julie snaps.

'Put that down, Alex. These bones belonged to real people.' I hate that he's being so disrespectful.

'Oh, come on, don't be so serious.' Alex holds up the skull and pretends to talk to it. 'You'd make a nice little reading lamp, monsieur. I think I will have to take you home.'

'That skull didn't belong to a man,' I say. 'It's too small. It's from a child around our age. She or he died of an infectious disease. Probably leprosy.' Alex drops the skull. It hits the bone-covered floor and splinters.

'Did you see the scarred bone under the eye socket?' I point out. 'It's a typical sign.'

'D-d-does anyone have hand sanitiser?' Alex stutters.

'You won't catch leprosy from a skull. These bones are hundreds of years old. There's no bacteria left on them.'

Julie looks at me. 'Are you sure?'

'Yes, I read it.'

'How many books do you read a week?' Alex asks.

'Last week I read three,' I reply, 'including one on archaeology and the catacombs. There's a lot you can tell from bones and skulls. For instance, lesions on the vertebra often point to Malta fever. That's a bacterial infection you can get from drinking unpasteurised milk.'

'You're amazing,' Julie says. 'You know so much.'

Has she forgotten about the Allosaurus and all the other things I used to tell her? 'I've always been this way. I haven't changed,' I say. *You did,* I think to myself. *And I don't know why.* As if she can hear me anyway, Julie looks away from me.

We crawl for a while in silence. Then walk. There are no bones left anymore, just mud and water. It splashes around my ankles. Suddenly, a shriek echoes through the tunnels.

'I can't see!' Julie is somewhere behind Alex and me, but the tunnel around her is pitch black. Her torch has gone out.

I move my head until my torch beam finds her. She throws up a hand in front of her face, blinded. 'I CAN'T SEE!' she screams.

I look up a bit, directing my light out of her eyes. Alex points his torch at the wall next to her. Julie blinks at us, her face pinched. Her fear is even more unexpected than Alex's was. I don't know what to say. Judging by the long silence, neither does Alex.

'So ... yeah,' Julie laughs shakily, stuffing her hair behind her ears. 'I'm kind of afraid of the dark.'

'Really?' I can't imagine Julie being scared of anything.

She shrugs, wandering closer into our bubble of light. 'I guess so. I mean, I always was as a kid. And now we're down here, totally reliant on torches to see – aren't *you* scared?'

When I shake my head, my torchlight draws zigzags in the air.

'Not of the *dark*,' Alex says carefully.

'But …' Julie draws a deep breath. 'What if all our torches died? How would we ever find our way out?

'That's extremely unlikely,' I say. 'My LED head torch lasts for 30,000 hours. We'll be out way before then.' Julie nods. The data seems to comfort her as it does me.

'Here, take this.' Alex hands her his torch.

'Are you sure?' I can tell she really wants to take it.

He nods.

'Thanks, Alex. How far are we from the World War II bunker, Hugo?'

'Two kilometres. We should be there soon,' I reply. 'Wait, where is that music coming from?'

'What music?' Alex asks.

'MC Solaar. French hip hop from the 1990s. My mum says he's a poet.'

'Spy, what I mean is, I don't hear any music.'
Julie closes her eyes. 'Neither do I.'

'I often hear stuff that other people don't,' I
say. Like the humming of a bee metres away.
Or Mum's 'silent' dishwasher, which may be
silent for neurotypicals but not for me. I think
they should hire autistic people to develop
silent household appliances. We're the experts,
after all.

From the dark tunnel we step into another,
larger gallery filled with beautiful, bright
murals. Someone has painted two waves
on a wall, a big one on top and a smaller
one beneath. Cataphiles call this place *La
Plage*, which means 'The Beach'. The wave
crests remind me of lion claws, but it's not
the paintings that draw my attention. It's the
people.

We've found the cataphiles.

LA PLAGE

A group of people are dining on canned tuna, beans and baguettes at a makeshift table in the middle of the cavern, sipping red wine from plastic cups. I take a step backwards into Alex and Julie.

MC Solaar roars from loudspeakers. At the back of the room, a woman juggles five brightly coloured rings. A man with orange locs paints an octopus on a piece of the wall that's still blank. When the cataphiles see us, they look as surprised as I feel. The juggler turns the music off. That's better.

'Hello,' I say, hesitantly. I can't believe I'm finally getting to meet some cataphiles.

'Did you run away from pre-school or something?' the orange-haired painter says, prompting laughter from the group as they recover.

'We're actually in Year 8,' I explain. How could he think we're under five years old? He must not have kids of his own.

'We come in peace,' Alex adds, forking his fingers solemnly.

A woman gets up from the table. She's wearing a dirty blue jumpsuit. Her dark hair is tied in a ponytail.

'First time in the underground?' she asks.

We all nod.

'I'm Cassandra. We come here every weekend to have fun.' She lights a cigarette. The smoke makes my nose itch. We introduce ourselves. Then she waves to the man with locs at the back of the gallery.

'Kaos! Some initiates for you!'

'I'll just finish the octopus,' Kaos says, not turning around.

'Are these the cataphiles?' Julie whispers.

She sounds doubtful, which I understand. They don't seem as friendly as I'd imagined. Maybe I should break the ice and tell them that I've been looking for them. That I'm here in the underground to look for Philibert's bottle, and that eventually I'll give it to them.

But something tells me it's better to stay silent.

Cassandra invites us to join them at the makeshift table. Alex wolfs down a tin of tuna. I'm too nervous to eat. I'm crammed between Cassandra and a man with a shaved head named Beowulf.

There's something strange about those names. Kaos. Cassandra. Beowulf. And what did Cassandra mean by 'initiates'?

Beowulf leans forwards and whispers in my ear. His breath smells of coffee and cigarettes.

'Have you met the Green Devil yet?'

I say nothing. I don't want to talk about the Green Devil now. I still haven't decided for myself if he's real or not.

Beowulf smiles, showing crooked teeth.

Then he turns, revealing the tattoo on the back of his shaved head. The Green Devil!

'I once saw him sneaking around Philibert Aspairt's tombstone,' Beowulf whispers, turning back. 'He disappeared before I could take a picture of him.'

Kaos, the orange-haired painter, appears from behind us and grabs Beowulf by the shoulder. 'Don't listen to this guy,' he tells me. 'He's crazy. Too much time in the underground. He hasn't seen sunlight in two years.'

'That's because I'm a creature of the dark!' Beowulf declares.

'That's scientifically impossible,' I point out. 'Humans need sunlight because it produces vitamin D, a molecule that our bodies don't produce on their own.' In scary times I like to go back to the certainty of science. Maybe I should apply that principle to the Green Devil too. He can't be real. It's just not possible.

'Know-it-all,' Beowulf mumbles.

'Who's the leader of your group?' Kaos asks suddenly.

Julie's eyes find mine across the table. If being the leader means being knowledgeable about the underground, that would be me. But how can I explain our trio's complicated dynamic to Kaos in just a few sentences? Turns out, I don't need to.

'That's me.' Alex gets up, wipes his mouth with his sleeve and extends his hand.

'Not yet.' Kaos pushes Alex's hand away. 'What's your cave name?'

'What?'

'Everyone has a cave name down here,' Cassandra explains, opening another can of tuna. 'A name that we only use in the underground. We're not the same people here that we are on the surface, where we leave our real names behind. Think of it as taking off a mask.'

'Down here we reveal our true nature,' Kaos whispers with an air of mystery. I don't think I like their true natures. They're so different from how I imagined cataphiles being.

Kaos drags Alex to the middle of the gallery.

'You too,' Kaos says, pointing at me until I join them. He opens a can of baked beans and hands it to me. What does he want me to do with it?

'Empty it over his head!'

'What?' Alex jerks.

'Why?' I'm confused. 'What is this?'

'It's just a harmless initiation ceremony. Everyone has to go through it. Welcome to the underground, guys!' Cassandra laughs and raises her plastic cup in a toast.

For me, memories are more than just increasingly vague impressions of the past. Whenever I remember something, detailed images pop into my mind. I usually know what day of the week it was and whether it was raining or not. My brain is making a biography of my life, one that replays automatically the moment I'm reminded of certain scenes. That can be great. But not all of my memories are pleasant. Like the one that starts replaying now. Like Thursday afternoon, January 7th ...

It was an unusually warm winter day that almost felt like spring. There wasn't a cloud in the sky, only vapour trails left behind by aeroplanes. Alex and some kids from our class were sitting outside, on the big lawn in front of the school. It was lunchtime. A couple of boys were playing football. I didn't play because I couldn't tell my team members apart from the opposition. It often happens when there are too many people in the same place: they end up all looking the same to me. So I just sat nearby on my own, reading a book about maps. Everything was fine, until it wasn't.

I could feel cold liquid dripping down my eyelashes, the sweetness of milk blending with my salty tears. I remember the flooded pages of my book. I remember Alex's laughter ...

'No. I won't do that,' I say, handing the can of baked beans back to Kaos.

I watch Alex's face. Expressions flit across it almost too quickly for me to catch. Fear? Humiliation? Disbelief?

'Whatever,' Kaos says. Then he empties the

can over Alex's head himself. The only sound in the cavern is Julie's gasp, amplified by her hands covering her mouth and nose. The beans slide down Alex face in slow motion, creating a mask of lumpy tomato sauce.

'May these beans seal your membership to the order of the cataphiles!' Kaos declares solemnly. 'And make sure to get yourself a cave name real quick.'

'What about X-Man?' Cassandra grins, pointing to Alex's legs. He tries to hide it with baggy trousers, but Alex is a little knock-kneed. That means that his knees tilt together while his feet stay quite far apart – making an X shape.

Cassandra's suggestion is met with applause and laughter.

'You're next,' Kaos says. He means me.

These aren't my people.

This isn't where I belong.

Where is the cataphile spirit that Claudine was talking about? The lack of judgment? The equality? Not here. This is the same as school. It's just that the milk has been traded for a can of baked beans. I watch one glide down Alex's cheek and fall towards his feet in slow motion. I feel the meltdown coming in reverse, crawling up my spine at top speed.

Thoughts I'll only find words for later flood my mind. *I came all this way to find a place where I would finally fit in. To find friends who would finally understand me. You're not them! You're not true cataphiles! You just a bunch of grown-ups behaving like school kids!*

Dazzling white light narrows my vision. Electricity runs over my body like the third rail on a train track. An autistic adult once told me that for her a meltdown feels like being swarmed by bees, each speaking to her in a different language. For me it's my mind itself that buzzes and hums. I feel the essence of my emotions: the anger, the humiliation, and most of all the disappointment – pure and razor-sharp. It takes my breath away.

Kaos touches my arm, and the slight pressure is too much. I erupt. I grab a bottle of wine from the table and throw it. Alex ducks.

The bottle shatters against a stone wall, washing the octopus with red.

'Don't touch me!' I scream.

Kaos jumps back from the spray of liquid and glass. 'Are you out of your mind?' he yells.

Yes. I am. Right at this moment, I've lost control of my words and actions.

I feel helpless.

Snot runs down my throat. Hot tears stream down my cheeks. I don't know what happens next. For a few minutes, my brain is a blizzard. When I feel a meltdown approaching in school, I leave the room before it hits. When Alex drenched me in milk, I ran away and banged my head on a toilet cubicle door. When things get too intense for me during class, I retreat into the room next door and rest on my red beanbag. But here, in a gallery twenty metres below Paris, I'm exposed.

I sink to the ground and bury my head in my hands, looking to create a barrier between the stressors and my brain. After a moment, I feel something warm and light covering my head and shoulders. I don't know what it is and my mind is too busy to focus on it. All I know is that it adds to the barrier, and it doesn't set me off like Kaos's touch did.

I go through the maps that are stored in my head. I follow our journey from the moment I entered the underground to where we have arrived now. I repeat this over and over, resetting my brain.

For a while, I can't hear anything beyond my safe space. Then, slowly, I can hear voices again. Finally, I can attach names to them, and they don't belong to Alex or Julie.

I pull my protective cover away and realise it's Julie's jacket that she has draped over me. The voices belong to Beowulf and Kaos. They're whispering loudly to each other. They look alarmed.

'Thank you,' I tell Julie, handing back her jacket.

'You're welcome,' she says. 'Are you OK?'

Before I can answer, Beowulf shoves Kaos, and Cassandra jumps to her feet.

'Let's move it!' she barks.

Within seconds they disappear into the darkness, without their equipment and without any goodbyes. The floor is littered with empty cans, cups and wine bottles. They didn't bother to clean up.

Did my meltdown make them flee?

As my senses continue to return, I hear footsteps. The static of a walkie-talkie. Two men wearing orange helmets step into the gallery. They look like Cassandra and her friends – wearing wellies and head torches – but the writing on their blue jumpsuits sets them apart:

'POLICE'.

ON THE RUN

'Police! Stay where you are! You're trespassing.'

'This way!' Julie shouts, grabbing my hand.

In normal times, I would never run from the police. But we're not supposed to be down here, and I'm not thinking clearly. Instinct takes over as we stumble through tunnels and galleries, past colourful graffiti and murals. I'm still tired from the meltdown. The more tired I am the more trouble I have locating my body in space, and the more difficult it is not to bump into things or trip over them, until I feel like a ping-pong ball bouncing through the tunnels. Alex isn't much better. At one point we both trip and end up in a heap together.

'Sorry!' we gasp, before we pull each other up and continue.

The police are fast on our heels. We veer left, right and back again. Our shoes crunch over rocks, our torch beams slash the darkness. I've lost track of our route, like a frozen navigation system, only the screen is stuck because we don't have permission to see the rest. We don't have a permit.

The lack of a focal point makes me very aware of the immensity of the underground network, with its endless tunnels and caverns, spanning beneath the city like a spiderweb. I think of Earth, the solar system, our galaxy, the ever-expanding universe – and me, a tiny dot within it.

I feel light-headed. I need walls, borders, limits. And then I see another of Guillaumot's inscriptions. My system resets itself, like a satnav rebooting. I know where we are.

'Damn! I can't see anything!'

A voice echoes through the tunnels. One of the police officer's head torches must have gone out. It's just the opportunity we need. We run for a while longer, then stop.

'We lost them,' I whisper. 'It's OK.'

'Why are we even running?' Alex gasps. 'They can help us.'

'Or blame us for the fresh graffiti and littering back there,' Julie points out. 'You want that on your criminal record?'

'They won't give us a record for that!'

'Just a fine for the trespassing!'

At the mention of the fine, Alex shuts up.

While we catch our breath, I notice Alex and Julie glancing at me, obviously trying to decide if I'm still in bottle-throwing mode.

'I'm OK now,' I tell them. 'When the pressure is too much, I need to release it. It's not something I can control. I say things. I throw stuff.' I pause. 'I'm really sorry, Alex. I wasn't trying to hit you.'

'It's OK,' he mumbles. 'I understand.'

I don't know if he does, but hopefully he's trying. More people should try. When I was little, Mum bought me a T-shirt that said

'I'm not misbehaving, I'm autistic. Please be understanding.' Some people were. Others accused her of being a bad mother. I refused to wear that shirt after a while.

I wish I could say that I don't get embarrassed after meltdowns anymore. Mathilde says I shouldn't, and I agree with her. But she agreed with *me* that what is and what should be are two very different things.

'I know!' Alex says suddenly. 'The Incredible Hulk! That's who you can dress as for the fancy dress party!'

'That's not fair, Alex,' Julie says. 'It's not his fault he acts out like that.'

'I'm *not* acting out,' I insist.

'"I've got a problem. There are aspects of my personality that I can't control!"'

Alex says this in the Hulk's voice. Whenever the Hulk gets angry, he turns green and spins out of control. A bit like me. Except I don't change colour, and I don't develop superhuman strength. I have none of the good elements of the Hulk meltdown – like being able to throw cars in the air and catch the bad guys. I'm only left with the anger, embarrassment … and loneliness.

Tears come into my eyes.

'That was a bad joke,' Alex says quickly. 'I was trying to lighten the mood. Sorry.' He pats my back. 'And thanks for not emptying the beans over my head yourself back there.'

'Why would I? And why would you? The milk, I mean.' It still doesn't make any sense to me.

Alex looks away abruptly. 'I don't remember. It was a long time ago.' A baked bean slides off his head. 'Gross,' he mutters, trying to shake more off.

'You have some on your shoulder too,' I say.

'Oh.' Alex briskly runs his hand over his left shoulder.

'No, the other one. Wait. Let me get them for you.' I pick off two beans near the base of his neck.

'And here.' Julie picks a bean out of the back of Alex's hair.

'Wait a minute! What is this? Social grooming? You're making me feel like a chimpanzee!' Alex laughs. It's a different laugh to the one I've heard so often lately, usually at my expense. Far from looking like a chimpanzee, Alex just looks happy.

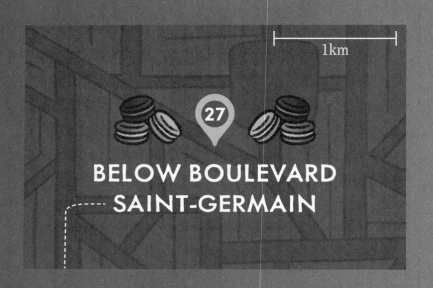

BELOW BOULEVARD SAINT-GERMAIN

'Look! We're below *Boulevard Saint-Germain*,' Julie says, pointing to a chiselled inscription in the wall. The underground really is the mirror image of the city streets above; its darker doppelgänger. It's a place where we lose the masks we wear in everyday life. Alex isn't that brave. Julie isn't that perfect – or so she says.

We must be very close to the World War II bunker now. The *Lycée Montaigne*, whose basement is connected to the bunker, is located at *17 Rue Auguste Comte*, just across from the *Jardin de Luxembourg*.

BLVD SAINT-GERMAIN

JARDIN DE
LUXEMBOURG

Another ten minutes and we should be there. Alex checks his watch. I don't think he's given up the idea of joining his mum for their Tuesday night lasagne.

Suddenly, I hear music again. I've become so used to the silence down here that what should only be faint sounds in the background now make me feel like I'm standing next to a concert stage. But it doesn't irritate me. I like it.

'Follow me,' I say. The music is soft and soothing. I want to get closer to it. I can hear voices now too.

We reach a large cavern crammed with people. Beige stone glows in the warm flicker of candles that sit in niches carved into the walls. There are no tuna cans and plastic cups here. Waiters in fancy uniforms serve tiny crab sandwiches and salmon canapés topped with mayonnaise and cucumber. A jazz band plays in the back corner. One of the musicians caresses the drums with a brush that looks like Mum's eggbeater, producing a soft rustling sound almost like white noise. Everything here looks neater and prettier than it did at Cassandra's place. Less improvised.

The Green Devil stands at a high table and holds a glass of orange juice. His left horn has come off and the glue is still visible on his forehead. His true skin colour shines through the green paint around his nose. And is that mayonnaise on his cheek?

'Oh, hi,' the Green Devil greets us, wiping his mouth with a green napkin and smearing more face paint. 'We met earlier, didn't we?'

My mouth hangs open. I don't know what to say.

'I'm Richard.' He grins and shakes my limp hand. 'I tried to tell you that before, but you ran away.'

'We thought you were chasing us!' Julie says.

'So ... you're *not* a devil?' I ask, touching his sticky forehead. I need to make sure he's really human.

'No. I'm a lawyer. I didn't mean to scare you, I just wanted to make sure you were OK.'

Alex bursts out laughing. 'You didn't scare

me! I didn't buy it for a second. Unlike my friend here.' I jump as Alex claps me suddenly on the back. Did he just say 'friend'?

'*He* thought you were real,' Alex tells Richard.

'What's up with your eyes?' I ask, still trying to make sense of it all.

'Green contacts,' Richard says, almost apologetically. 'I can't wait to take them out. My eyes are itching like mad. Charlotte insisted I wear them. But, hey, what can you do when your best friend asks you to dress up as the Green Devil for her book launch party?'

Next to the jazz band I see a promotional poster with a picture of a hand reaching out from a manhole. I immediately recognise the cover of the graphic novel I saw at the book store.

THE GREEN DEVIL.

'Who's Charlotte?' Julie asks.

'Charlotte Doucet. The bestselling author of *The Green Devil*!'

A blonde-haired woman in a purple polka-dot dress signs books at a round party table.

Her lips are red and she wears her hair in a bun that looks messy and elegant at the same time. I can't believe someone so friendly-looking, with such a soft-sounding name, would write about something as scary as the Green Devil.

'So,' Richard continues more seriously, 'what are you guys doing down here? I'm guessing you don't have a permit.' I must look alarmed because he immediately puts his hand on my shoulder. 'Don't worry, I won't tell anyone.'

'Do *you* have a permit?' Alex counters.'

'Of course,' Richard says. 'The publisher took care of everything. Charlotte just sold the film rights to a big Hollywood studio. Hence the salmon canapés. Are you guys hungry? Thirsty?' Without waiting for an answer, he hands us each a glass of orange juice. Alex helps himself to six small sandwiches, while Julie and I nibble on green macarons filled with pistachio mousse. On top of each macaron sits a tiny devil made of green almond paste.

'Ladurée made them especially for the launch,' Richard informs us. They're delicious.

Charlotte's Hollywood deal must be quite something. Not everyone can afford custom-made macarons by Ladurée.

I wipe my mouth and I move towards Charlotte's autograph table.

'I like your dress,' I tell her. 'The chest pockets have sixteen dots each.'

'I know!' Charlotte grins.

'Did you count them too?' I'm surprised that other people do that.

'Of course. I count everything. It relaxes me. There are 156 dots on the entire dress, by the way. What are you guys doing down here in the underground? You're not lost, are you?' She frowns briefly.

'No,' I say truthfully, 'I know the way out.'

'We're just exploring,' Julie say, slightly less truthfully.

'It's amazing, right? Richard and I hung out down here every weekend when we were teenagers. That was before the internet. Not that many people knew about the place – it was all word of mouth. Today it's filled with tourists from all over the world. Imagine that!'

'Amazing,' I agree. I like Charlotte. She's just the kind of cataphile I imagined meeting: so passionate about the underground that she set her first book here.

'Of course,' Charlotte adds, 'exploring the underground in a tour group of strangers isn't the same. Richard and I have been friends since childhood – just like you three!'

My heart skips a beat. I want to stop time and cover my ears, afraid that Alex or Julie will tell her that she's wrong – that we aren't friends.

Instead, they both smile.

Just like that, everything I'd hoped for becomes reality – here, twenty metres below Paris, at a book party with a fake Green Devil and a graphic novel writer, eating ham with cucumber and mayonnaise canapés. The world is instantly brighter, the tiny little devils atop the macarons turn greener, and Charlotte's dress reminds me of a lavender field in full bloom, punctuated by 156 black bumblebees.

'All the people in this room are my friends,' Charlotte says. 'I met many of them underground, but our friendship continued on the surface.'

I hope it will be the same for Alex, Julie and me.

But first, I need to get the bottle of chartreuse.

'Are you going to write another book?' Julie asks Charlotte.

'Oh yes! And it'll be set down here again. My publisher doesn't want me to talk about it yet. All I can tell you is that it involves a gang of jewellery thieves. No more green devils for me!' Charlotte laughs.

'Just when I was getting used to contact lenses,' Richard chuckles, reappearing with no horns at all now.

'It's going to be a proper detective story,' Charlotte continues. 'I had such a lot of fun researching the World War II bunker. That's where the thieves are hiding the stolen jewels before leaving the underground.'

I nod. 'It's the perfect choice,' I agree, 'with direct access to the *Lycée Montaigne's* basement. Speaking of which, we have to go. We're on a mission.'

'You're quite an expert, Hugo!' Charlotte declares. 'And very mysterious. I take it this isn't your first visit to the underground?'

'It is, but he knows *everything* about it,' Alex says, wolfing down his eleventh macaron. That's the nicest thing he's said about me in 307 days, since I told him about Carhenge in Nebraska. It's a replica of Stonehenge made out of thirty-nine vintage American cars instead of standing stones. Alex said he wanted to go there with me one day.

'It was great to meet you, and sorry I scared you!' Richard puts his hand on my shoulder, stamping a green mark on my jacket.

'Here, take this,' Charlotte hands me her business card. 'Call me when you're back home. I'll send you guys signed copies of the book. That way you don't have to carry them around now. Especially since you're on a mission.'

She winks at me. We wave goodbye, taking a last look at the book party, with Charlotte and Richard and their friends.

I've finally met them. *True cataphiles.*

As we leave the party, Alex suddenly stops in his tracks. 'Wouldn't it be better if we leave the underground now and send the police to the World War II bunker? I mean, even if Hugo's right and the stolen bottles are there, what are we supposed to do with them?'

'Good point,' Julie says. 'We could leave now and give the police an anonymous tip-off so we don't get in trouble.'

'No!' I say. 'I have to find the chartreuse.'

'Why?' Julie asks, confused.

I'm not sure they'll understand, but I have to tell them.

'I came underground because I wanted to find the chartreuse and give it to the cataphile community. Philibert is their patron saint and Claudine, the librarian who told me about it, said that nobody else had been able to find it. I wanted to find it so that I could become friends with the cataphiles. Because I didn't have any friends on the surface.'

Alex and Julie are staring at me.

Julie bites her lip. 'We're your friends, Hugo. I was wrong.'

'I know,' I say, even as my insides glow at the confirmation. 'And that's why now I just want to give the bottle to Claudine. Without her map, I wouldn't be here. And we wouldn't be friends again.'

I wait for Julie to say something else, but Alex surprises me.

'Sounds like a good enough reason to me,' he says. 'Lead the way, Hugo.'

It's the first time in 200 days that he's called me by my real name.

THE FLOODED TUNNEL

I don't stop at junctions to check for signs —
I know the way. In five minutes, we'll be under
the *Lycée Montaigne*, Zoé's school. That's where
we'll enter the World War II bunker.

The ceiling of the tunnel drops lower as we
continue. Eventually we have to crawl. My
mouth is dry from the dust of the limestone,
my eyes sting. Just as I become used to
navigating this part of the underground like
a reptile, the landscape changes again. The
ceiling gets higher and higher until we can
walk straighter, first with bent necks and then
completely upright. From out of nowhere,
water reappears. First it splashes around our

ankles, but after a few metres it's on the verge of spilling over Julie's wellies. Alex wades ahead up to his thighs before turning back.

'Looks like we'll have to swim.'

'This wasn't on my maps,' I blurt out.

'Where does all this water come from, anyway?' Julie asks, eyeing the little waves threatening to breach her wellies as Alex wades back to dry ground.

'Some parts of the underground are permanently flooded,' I say, trying to soothe myself with facts. 'Others fill up when it rains a lot. The water can be one and a half to two metres deep.'

'You need to start updating your maps, Hugo,' Alex says, pointedly pulling off his soggy trainers and then the hip waders. He slides into the water, swearing.

'Come on! What are you waiting for?' Julie's up to her waist now, too, while I stand back and eye the murky grey water.

'He can't swim.' Alex answers Julie's question.

'Yes, I can!' I retort.

I take off my waders so that they don't fill with water, leaving them behind like Alex did. I glide, shuddering, into the cold pool and try to keep my rucksack above the surface, hoping that the waterproofing claims were accurate.

'How come you almost drowned, then?' Alex asks, now swimming ahead of us.

'What?' Tentacles of hair spiral around Julie as she turns her head to look at me with wide eyes. 'Really?'

'No,' I say firmly. 'I just went under water.'

'Yeah,' Alex snorts, 'for like a really long time.'

'I was holding my breath. I can do it for a long time. The swimming teacher overreacted. I was just getting away from ...' I glance at Alex as he reaches the other side first. I remember the chants of *Go, Spy, go!*, and I don't finish the sentence.

'Me,' Alex says, surprising me. 'He was getting away from me.'

'Why?' Julie asks.

Alex is out of the water now. He removes his jacket and shrugs his wet shoulders. 'Because I was being a jerk.'

'Why?'

Another shrug. 'Because I *am* a jerk.'

'Why?' This time it's me asking.

'Mum says I'm angry.'

'About what?'

'Everything.' Alex looks up having wrung his hoodie into a croissant. 'I'm sorry, Hugo.'

I nod because I don't really know what to say. I notice his bare arm. 'Your tattoo's gone.'

Alex quickly rolls down his sleeve. *Water soluble. I knew it.*

Alex checks his watch again.

'6 p.m. I'm going to miss the lasagne.'

'Your mum can reheat it,' I offer.

'Not everyone has a stay-at-home mum, Hugo. Mine has two jobs. Friday is her only free evening. It's *our* evening.'

I consider this. My mum is always around when I need her, but my dad works a lot. I try to imagine him being my only parent. I try to imagine not having a sister at all. But I can't. And suddenly I'm as eager as Alex is to go home, to see them.

'We'll be out of here by 7,' I promise.

THE WORLD WAR II BUNKER

We're walking through the tunnel that leads to the World War II bunker. My wet jeans are chafing me. I don't just *hear* the squelching of my boots, without the waders on I *feel* it – like dirty sponges sucking at the soles of my feet, making my skin crawl. As well as a shower, I'd like a bowl of Mum's chicken soup with boiled eggs, chopped parsley and vermicelli *now*.

'Would anyone like to hear some map facts?' I offer, mostly to distract myself.

'M-me,' Julie's teeth chatter. 'I always liked your map facts – especially the Allo-s-s-saurus.'

She smiles at me, although it looks more like a grimace. Even Alex has his hands under his armpits as he looks at me and shrugs.

'Did you know,' I say, feeling suddenly warmer, 'that our maps of the moon are more detailed than our maps of the seafloor? It's because we can't use the same techniques we use on land for mapping. But knowing the seafloor is super important, since oceans cover 71% of the surface of the Earth. So to map the seafloor, they use this special tool called an echo-sounder,' I explain. 'Over 96.5% of the Earth's water is found in the oceans.'

'And the rest?' Alex asks.

'Lakes, rivers,' I say.

'And swimming pools,' Julie says, laughing. A few seconds later, her face changes. She doesn't smile anymore.

'I guess I forgot that there was a world outside of the swimming pool,' she admits. 'I really like the kids on my swimming team, you know. We spend so much time together. We go through lots of intense stuff. Like breaking records, winning championships and losing them. Sharing the same passion creates strong friendships. For Charlotte, it was the underground; for me, it's swimming.'

'That makes sense,' I say.

I check my watch. It's 6.15 p.m. The underground makes you lose all sense of time. There are no sunrises or sunsets, no changes in temperature. Everything stays the same, at a constant fifteen degrees Celsius. But the fifteen degrees feel more like five degrees now, with our wet clothes clinging to our bodies. It's time to bring this expedition to an end.

The World War II bunker is a huge labyrinth of rooms and corridors. Finding the bags of wine in it will be like looking for a needle in a haystack – except that any haystack is much safer than this place right now.

We slide into the bunker through an iron door. Minutes later, we pop out into the *Salle des Fresques*, a large gallery with graffitied walls. On one wall, an Aztec warrior tames a dragon. On the next, an astronaut holds the US flag.

We leave the gallery and step into a maze of corridors with concrete floors and arrows on the walls. A blue arrow points towards *Boulevard Saint-Michel*. A black one points towards *Notre Dame*. Nazi efficiency left over from the war.

Suddenly, we hear voices, faint and in the distance. I put one finger to my mouth. Julie nods. My heart pounds in my throat. We tiptoe through the corridor. I grab the handle of a rusty door. It opens with a creaking sound and leads to an empty room. I gasp. *Almost* empty.

'The bags!' Alex cries. They're the same ones the Vaders carried when they left us duct-taped in the wine cellar.

'The chartreuse must be in one of them,' I say. 'Come on, help me find it!'

I rush to open the bags, quickly scanning the contents. Alex and Julie squat down on the floor next to me. Each bag is filled with expensive-looking bottles with gold and silver labels and exotic-sounding names: Romanée-Conti. Puligny-Montrachet. But no chartreuse. Where is it? We still have one bag to check when we hear footsteps, although it's impossible to tell from where.

'We have to go,' Julie says, panicked.

'Just one more bag,' I say.

'I found it!' Alex exclaims. In his hands is the dusty bottle with the initials P.A., 1793. The voices down the hall become louder. Alex gives me the chartreuse and I put it in my rucksack. We run back to the door. Now we just have to follow the black arrows to get out of this maze. They'll guide us out, towards *Notre Dame*.

We fly past old metal doors, hanging from their hinges. Past a stall with a rusty chemical toilet. Past walls plastered with electric cables and fuse boxes. My lungs are on fire, and I'm not sure how long I can keep going. I've run more in the past five hours than I have in my life. Plus I had a meltdown. I'm tired.

Finally, I spot the black arrow. At a junction, we take the left corridor. We continue, passing doors and walls with German words on them. 'Entgiftung'. 'Notausgang'. 'Ruhe!' There's one phrase I recognise: 'Rauchen verboten'. ('No smoking'.) The wine thieves haven't complied with that order. The air is heavy with the smell of cigarette smoke mixed with garlic. At the end of the corridor, I see two men wearing black leather – and no masks. One is tall and thin, with a mole on the tip of his nose.

'It's the Vaders!' Julie whispers, interrupting me before I can make out the other man.

I push her and Alex into a room on my right. 'Verhörungsraum' says the sign on the door. I'm not fluent in German, but I have a feel

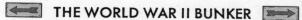

for languages. Sometimes, when I examine words, they reveal their personality to me. 'Schreibmaschinenraum' looks very friendly. 'Verhörungsraum', on the other hand, looks threatening. Like a Nazi officer in uniform, clicking the heels of his tall, black leather boots. Maybe it's the ö. I never liked umlauts.

30
THE VERHÖRUNGSRAUM

I close the door behind us and scan the dingy room we're in. In the middle of a concrete floor is a wooden table. An old-fashioned telephone hangs on the wall. There's nothing else.

'Let's just wait a couple of minutes until they're gone,' I say, checking my watch. 'It's 6.30 p.m. You're going to make it for your mum's lasagne, Alex.'

Alex gives me a high-five. He always used to do that.

'What about you, Julie? Do you have to be home at a particular time?' I ask.

'No. And I'm not in a rush.'

'Why's that?'

'My parents have separated.' Julie says it matter-of-factly.

'Divorced, you mean?' Alex asks.

'No, the bit before the divorce. For a divorce you need lawyers and paperwork. Separating is less complicated. My dad just left.'

'I'm really sorry to hear that.' I wonder how it must feel when one parent leaves. 'My dad is gone a lot for work, but he always comes back.'

'It's probably my fault,' Julie says.

'It's not your fault. Parents don't separate because of their kids. They do it because of themselves,' Alex says.

'How do you know?' I ask. I want to know his sources – and why he suddenly sounds so wise.

'My dad left before I was born. He didn't even know me, so it's impossible for it to be my fault.'

I nod. 'That makes sense.'

'I don't know,' Julie says. 'My parents fought all the time. Now they're like, "We've drifted apart". And I'm like "Well, drift together again"! It can't be that difficult!'

'They're like Pangea,' I say.

'The supercontinent?'

'Yeah. Two hundred million years ago, all the continents were glued together. Then they started to drift apart, until they reached the positions we know today.'

'So you're saying Mum and Dad will never drift back together again?' Julie says.

'No! Your mum and dad are humans, not continents. Humans drift back together again all the time.'

'What makes you say that?'

'Well, *we* did.'

There's a beat of silence, then Julie smiles. 'Yeah,' she says, putting an arm across my shoulders and squeezing them. 'I guess we did.'

I press my ear against the door. It's silent beyond.

'It's safe to leave now,' I say, slowly opening the door. No Vaders in sight. No smell of chemical garlic. We step into the corridor and run towards the exit of the bunker. On the way to the manhole at *Boulevard Saint-Michel*, I tell Alex and Julie about how the brain can be mapped like a continent. About the paper towns: imaginary places that cartographers created to catch those who tried to copy their maps. Cartographers would add towns that didn't exist and if these towns appeared on someone else's map, they'd know that the new map was a copy of their own.

I tell them about the oldest star map on earth (an estimated 16 or 17,000 years old). It was found in the *Lascaux* cave in southwestern France, showing the stars Altair, Deneb and Vega – also known as the Summer Triangle, each the brightest star in its respective constellation.

I tell them about René Suttell and Jean Talairach, the two junior doctors who in 1943 mapped the underground in an effort to help

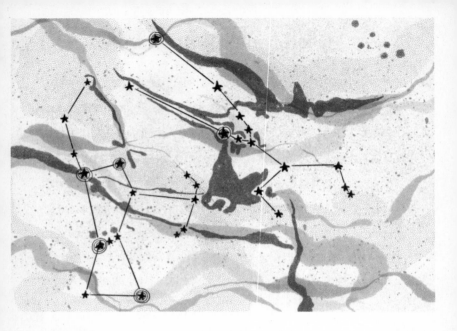

the French resistance during World War II. While Talairach was working at Sainte-Anne Hospital in Paris in 1938, he and his colleague, Suttell, found a secret door that led to the underground. Together they mapped the underground, with Talairach using points of reference such as manholes, inscriptions on the underground walls, doors, etc.

Thirty years later, using the same method of measuring the distance and angle between two points, Talairach created an atlas of the brain. It described the location of structures found

in every brain, no matter its size and overall shape. This atlas was especially important for brain surgeons before they had sophisticated instruments like CT scanners and MRIs.

Countries, continents. Skies, brains and train routes – it seems like everything can be mapped. I talk like I'm trying to squeeze each and every one into the little time we have left.

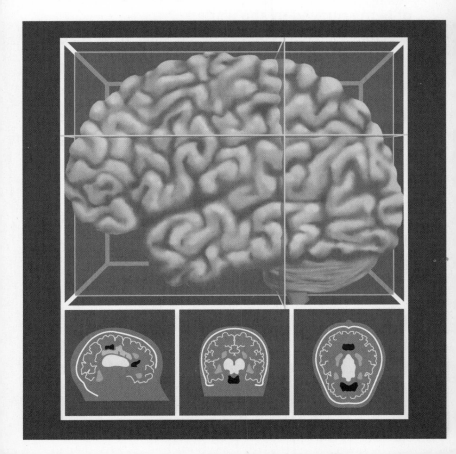

Alex and Julie listen to me without interrupting once. When we reach the manhole at *Boulevard Saint-Michel*, I know that our adventure has ended. What will happen once we reach the surface? Will they still listen to my stories, or will they go back to ignoring me?

Part of me wants to stay down here forever, for the quiet and the darkness, and the feeling of being hugged by the walls.

'Where is that light coming from?' Julie asks.

I look ahead and see a bright point in the distance, beyond the beams of our torches. 'It looks like the manhole by *Brasserie Splendid* is open.' Thank goodness. Remembering how heavy it was, I'm not even sure all three of us could have moved it.

I climb up the ladder, followed by Alex and Julie. The sounds of the street become louder as I go. I hear cars honking, dogs barking, people talking. We're approaching civilisation.

'What the devil?'

I look up and I see two men wearing hip waders, rubber gloves and wide-eyed

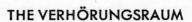

expressions below their helmets. '*Ville de Paris – Service des égouts*' is written in black letters on their overalls. Sewer workers!

'Not the devil,' I say, climbing out of the manhole. 'Just me.'

'And me,' says Julie, following.

'Boo,' Alex concludes.

I look up and I see the letter sign, sparkling in the early evening light like a million diamonds: '*Brasserie Splendid*'.

We made it. We're out.

And I have never craved a Dame Blanche more.

THE POLICE STATION

The sewer workers took us straight to the closest police station. Alex's mum, Julie's parents and Mum arrived soon after bearing dry clothes for each of us. The police gave us separate rooms for privacy: my room is simple, with a bare table and a clock that makes a loud, distracting ticking noise. On one grey wall hangs an Interpol poster with the headline 'Wanted Persons'.

Julie is with her parents in the room next to ours. There's a lot of talking going on and the police station's walls are thin. I might be able to understand what they're saying if they weren't speaking Mandarin.

Alex has already left with his mum. We didn't make it for 7 p.m., but Alex's mum looked so happy to see him that I think she'll make lasagne every day for the rest of his life if he wants.

Mum has been holding my hand for the past ten minutes. She was crying when she got here, and she hugged me for so long that I thought she'd never let go.

'Promise me you'll never do anything like this again,' she sniffs. Mascara has left black streaks down her cheeks; it clearly isn't waterproof.

'I promise,' I say. 'You can let go of my hand.'

The door opens and a woman with short black hair and a friendly smile enters the room. 'My name is Alice, I'm a police officer. Will you please follow me, Hugo?'

She guides me and Mum into another room that looks exactly like the one we've just been in. Julie and her parents are already there, along with a man. He's holding a sketchpad so he must be the artist in charge of composite sketches. I sit at the table next to Julie. Her eyes are red, but she looks happy.

'Are you ready?' Alice asks. When I nod, she adds, 'This is Marc, the forensic artist. He'll use what you say to put together a drawing of what the thieves look like.'

'We're ready to cooperate,' I say. 'But before we start, we want a guarantee that you won't charge us for illegally roaming the underground.' Alice assures us that she hadn't planned on doing that anyway.

'Or graffitiing,' Julie adds. 'Because that wasn't us.' Again, Alice promises that we're not in any trouble, and we won't get criminal records.

'Our team is combing through the bunker and the wine cellar right now,' she says. 'Monsieur Noiseau has been informed as well. So far we haven't recovered any of the bottles.'

I think of the chartreuse in my rucksack. I still want to give it to Claudine. She deserves it.

'You're here,' Marc takes over, 'because unlike your friend Alex, you both saw the thieves' faces. Do you think you can describe them to me?'

Julie shakes her head. 'No, I don't really remember anything. Just that one was tall and skinny.'

'How about you, Hugo?'

I close my eyes. The pictures that my brain took of the Vaders are firmly stored in my head. I describe Vader One, with his mole and his shaved head; Vader Two's curly hair. Plus anything else I can think of. When I open my eyes again, Marc's pencil is dancing across the page, their faces slowly taking shape.

'That's them!' I say when he's finished. 'That's exactly what they looked like!'

Julie is amazed. 'But Hugo, how did you …? I mean, we hardly saw them …'

'An estimated quarter of a second,' I say. 'That's usually enough for me. And you're right: Vader One was tall and thin, with bony hands that look like a spider. Vader Two was more compact with short arms and legs. Typical ectomorph and endomorph body types.'

Marc gives me a surprised look. 'Those are complicated words, Hugo.' They are. But I've read Mum's fitness book based on body types. Mum is an ectomorph, which means that she is tall and thin and needs to work with heavy weights.

'Will these sketches be enough to catch them?' Mum asks Alice. She's holding my hand again.

'It depends what other details we find out.'

'They also smelled of garlic,' I say. 'Not real garlic, though. More like synthetic garlic.'

Marc shoots me a puzzled look.

'What does synthetic garlic smell like?'

'Like real garlic, with a chemical note. I can't explain it.'

'That's OK,' Marc says, putting his pencil down. 'I can't draw smells anyway.'

'But what if it's important?'

'I'll make a note.' But he doesn't. He stands up to leave, and Mum finally lets go of me to 'have a chat' with Julie's parents. The words 'been a long time' and 'shame about the circumstances' drift back to us before they lower their voices.

I remember the last time Julie and I hung out at her house. She taught me how to bake Chinese butter biscuits, and afterwards my mum and dad sat with her mum and dad to taste test them. Because I love maps, we used a biscuit cutter in the shape of France. Together we iced them in red, white and blue. It was so much fun.

'Why did you drift away from me?' I ask suddenly.

Julie hesitates. 'I was busy with swimming,' she says. But then she shakes her head. 'No, that's not true. I mean, I was busy – I *am* busy – but that wasn't the real reason I didn't have time for you anymore. The real reason was that I'd become part of this whole new world, with all these cool sports kids, and championships, and trophies, and you ... you just didn't fit in that world with me.

'I couldn't hang out with you at home anymore because Mum and Dad were fighting. And I was afraid that if we hung out at school, my new friends wouldn't accept me, so …' Julie breathes out a long breath. 'So in the end I just ignored you. I was such a coward. I'm sorry.'

'Oh,' I say. I'm struck by the idea that I'm not the only one who worries about being accepted. Julie does too. Maybe even Alex. Then I'm struck by something else she said.

'… So I'm not cool?'

'No, *I'm* not, Hugo! You're the coolest kid above and below Paris. You always have been. Never mind your memory or your senses – to me your gift was making me smile back when I wanted to cry. You were a really good friend to me, and I was a really bad one to you. If you let me, I can't promise to be "perfect", but I really want to be better …'

She's looking at me like I might actually say no, and I realise then that I could. I could reject her. But I don't want to.

'OK,' I agree. 'You can be better.'

The following day, Dad calls from Narita airport near Tokyo. He had planned to stay in Japan until the weekend, but when Mum told him what happened he booked a flight home right away. I feel like I've been asleep since we left the police station. In fact, apart from a short shower and some tinned soup (I was too tired to wait for Mum to make hers), I have been. Mum even let me skip school.

'How are you feeling, Hugo?' Dad asks. 'Are you OK?'

In the background, I can hear the flight announcement in English and Japanese: *'Air France flight 275 with service to Paris Charles de Gaulle is now boarding at Gate 67. Please proceed to the gate and have your passports and boarding cards ready.'*

'I'm OK, don't worry,' I say. I'm more than OK, actually. I'm happy. I tell him about the thieves and the wine cellar, even though he's heard some of it from Mum. It's my favourite part of the underground adventure.

Dad chuckles. 'Darth Vader masks? We'll

never be able to watch *Star Wars* the same way again!'

'I'll never be able to eat Mum's garlic bread the same way either.'

'Why's that?'

'It'll remind me of the Vaders. They smelled like garlic. Chemical garlic.'

'Chemical garlic? You mean like rat poison?'

'… What?'

'I've used rat poison in our basement before and I thought the same thing. That stuff definitely smells like garlic. I wouldn't compare it to Mum's garlic bread, though – at least not in front of her!'

'Last call for Air France flight 275 to Paris,' a voice is now saying in the background.

'I need to go now, Hugo. I'll see you tomorrow.'

'Have a good flight, Dad.'

As I hang up the phone, Zoé hands me a thick cream-coloured envelope. It looks expensive. 'This came for you,' she says. 'No stamp. That means it was hand-delivered.'

I open it. Inside there's a beautiful beige

invitation card. At the top of the card '*L'Accord*', the name of Monsieur Noiseau's restaurant, is embossed in gold. Zoé tries to read it over my shoulder until I cover the invitation with my hand.

'I hate it when you do that,' I tell her.

'What does it say?' she asks unrepentantly.

'*Hon nutsuu kilpet restoran, kippaan,*' I reply in Kielppo. ('He's inviting us to his restaurant to say thank you.') '*Alex, Julie u moo,*' I add, just to confuse her more. (Meaning 'Alex, Julie and me'.)

It's been a while since we spoke our secret language, and I'm convinced Zoé has forgotten it. Maybe it's not cool now that she's a teenager. But Zoé surprises me.

'*Onu tetsu ka celebriksaa!*' ('You're like celebrities now!') she replies.

'You still speak Kielppo!' I say in French.

'Of course, I do. I'm still your sister!' Then she switches back. '*Kako hon uopalla zna rutsuu zovis?*' ('How did he know where you live?')

She means Chef Noiseau, and the answer is I don't know.

But I'm more interested in how he'll react when he hears what else I have to tell him – and the police.

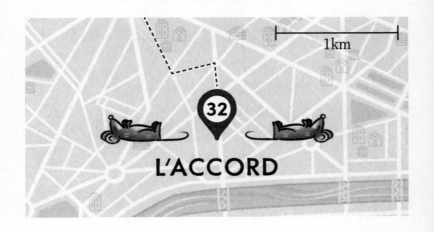

L'ACCORD

Two days later, I'm back at the police station – only I'm with Dad this time. Alice greets us with a wide grin and guides us to her office. Mum already shared the good news with me. They've identified the Vaders.

'We cannot thank you enough, Hugo. The description you gave helped us to arrest them. And you were right about the rat poison theory.'

'That was Dad's theory,' I correct her. 'I brought him today because he's the one who solved the last piece of the puzzle.'

'*You* solved it, Hugo. I only pointed you in the right direction,' Dad says.

'He's in the champagne business,' I say.

'He travels the world to tell people all about how great champagne tastes.'

'I guess that's my job description in a nutshell,' Dad says.

Alice is laughing. 'Well, you were *both* right about the rat poison. The Vaders set up a pest control firm to gain access to Noiseau's restaurant. It was all part of the theft.'

'Then you have all the evidence you need?' Dad asks her.

'We do. We even had their DNA on file.'

'So they're real criminals?' I ask. An uneasy, itchy feeling spreads through my body. Am I a criminal too if I give the chartreuse to Claudine instead of returning it?

'Petty criminals,' Alice replies. 'Mostly shoplifting, one car theft. This was definitely a step up. They claim they were acting on behalf of someone else – someone they never met, of course, so they couldn't give a description. According to them, they left the wine in the World War II bunker for this mystery client to collect, and that's why we haven't been able to locate it yet – because they don't know where it is.'

Alice scoffs softly. It's clear that she doesn't believe them about the mystery client. But I do. Emperor Palpatine. The list. The random bottles to *disguise* the list. It all makes sense. But who was it?

My brain churns as I stare into space.

'Hugo? Is everything all right?' Dad asks.

'Almost,' I mutter, distractedly. At least it will be once I've figured out who the Vaders were working for.

Everyone thinks the story is over. Everyone thinks the case is closed. But it's not. Not yet.

First, I have to meet Monsieur Noiseau.

I'm a bit nervous. In a couple of minutes, we're going to meet the most famous chef in Paris. I hope he won't file any trespassing charges against us. Maybe I should have asked Alice about that too.

A large, lit chandelier dangles from the ceiling (I count sixty-seven crystals before I see spots and have to look away); expensive-looking paintings hang on the walls. Philippe Noiseau has asked us to meet him at the 18th century townhouse that holds his world-famous restaurant, *L'Accord*. The mint-and-lemon water they serve us is refreshing. Alex asked for a cola first, but a waiter called Bertrand informed us that 'Monsieur Noiseau doesn't serve commercial soft drinks' because 'Monsieur Noiseau only believes in natural ingredients'.

We haven't met Monsieur Noiseau yet, but the way his employees talk about him tells me he's very respected, even revered. While we wait for the chef to arrive, Alex makes loud slurping noises and pokes at the mint leaves with the straw he requested, much to Bertrand's disgust.

Julie rolls her eyes. 'Alex! This is a three-star Michelin restaurant!'

'So? There's nobody around. Besides, it's a compliment. I'm only doing it because I really like this stuff. Tastes like peppermint chewing gum.' Alex reaches for a cream-coloured napkin on the next table over.

'Don't touch that!' Julie scolds, holding his hand back. 'They're getting ready to open and you'll ruin the table settings.'

'Fine,' Alex shrugs, wiping his mouth on his sleeve instead.

When Monsieur Noiseau finally walks into the large dining room, I feel a little starstruck. I guess that's because I've seen him on TV many times before. He's taller than I imagined. His name is embroidered in blue on his white chef uniform: 'Philippe Noiseau, *Restaurant L'Accord*'.

'So you're the kids from the wine cellar?' He greets us with a friendly grin. 'You have expensive tastes!' He sits at our table and nods at the waiter. Seconds later, a coffee appears.

'No, Monsieur, we're too young to drink alcohol,' I say. 'We would have drunk our own pee if we were stuck down there any longer, but thankfully that wasn't necessary.'

'That was a joke, Hugo,' Julie whispers to me.

'Oh.' I force a chuckle. 'That's funny.' I always feel a bit self-conscious when I don't get a joke.

'We're really sorry,' I say. 'I know we weren't supposed to be in there, but–'

'Oh no, not at all. In fact, I have to thank you,' the chef cuts me off, dropping a sugar cube into his coffee with silver tongs. 'You've identified the thieves. I'm confident the police will recover the wine any day now. Then they can close the investigation and I'll finally be allowed back in my cellar.'

'How much is the stolen wine worth, anyway?' Alex asks. A bit of mint leaf is stuck between his front teeth.

Monsieur Noiseau says, 'Oh, a few hundred thousand euros,'

I gasp.

'But some of the bottles are priceless, really,' Monsieur Noiseau continues. 'Have you ever heard of someone called Philibert Aspairt? He was the doorkeeper to the *Val-de-Grâce* military hospital and got lost in 1793 while trying to steal a bottle of chartreuse from an underground cellar.'

'They found his skeleton eleven years later, his keys still attached to his belt,' I finish for him, robotically. I can feel Alex and Julie eyeing me sidelong. Julie was the one who encouraged me to bring the chartreuse with us today.

'You should give it back,' she had said.

'You should sell it,' Alex had disagreed.

Now my heart pounds in my chest. My mind is turning like Mum's pasta machine, producing long, tangled thoughts like tagliatelle.

I should give the chartreuse to Claudine. Without her maps, I wouldn't have gone underground. And if I hadn't gone underground, Alex, Julie and I wouldn't be friends again.

Monsieur Noiseau looks surprised. 'You know Philibert's story?'

More importantly, so do you, I think. *And you're not talking about any other bottle. That must mean you know how special the chartreuse is. Are you really a cataphile too? I can't steal from another cataphile.*

The thought makes me itch on top of the growing guilt over stealing at all. It was one thing breaking rules when I was caught in the momentum of our underground adventure. Since then, I feel like the police officer's words for the Vaders are tattooed across my forehead: PETTY CRIMINAL.

I don't want to be a criminal – petty or otherwise. But how can I give the chartreuse back now?

'Hugo?'

'Yes!' I return to the conversation, nodding mechanically. 'Yes, I do. I know his story.'

Monsieur Noiseau takes a sip of his coffee, frowning as if it's not quite to his taste. On his next sip, I ask, 'Do you have any enemies, Monsieur?'

He coughs, spluttering coffee into his napkin. Was I too blunt? Mathilde told me that it's best to 'ease one's way into a conversation', but we don't have time for that now.

'Enemies?' The chef frowns, still dabbing his mouth. 'Not that I know of. Why?'

'The Vaders were working for someone.'

'That's what they're saying, yes. But there's no evidence it's true.'

'I think they're telling the truth. Can you tell me what happened after the rat infestation was discovered?' I ask. 'The Vaders came to see you, didn't they?'

Monsieur Noiseau's skin reddens as if I've slapped him. Bertrand the waiter arrives with a fresh napkin.

'That issue has been dealt with,' Bertrand says, and it sounds like something he's been repeating over and over again, to journalists and customers alike. 'No vermin have been seen at *L'Accord* since we hired pest controllers. Chef, should I show them the kitchen?'

'It's fine, Bertrand,' Monsieur Noiseau says. 'I'll handle it.'

Bertrand steps back, but he doesn't go away. I wonder if he doubles as Monsieur Noiseau's bodyguard. Finally, Monsieur Noiseau gives him a nod and he leaves reluctantly.

'You must excuse us,' Monsieur Noiseau

apologises. 'The words "rat infestation" bring back less than pleasant memories. You see a good reputation is like a good wine collection: it takes decades to build and moments to destroy.' He clears his throat.

'To answer your question, Hugo. Yes, the Vaders did approach me. Reports of rats in my restaurant had gone viral, and although I didn't believe them at the time, I had to do something.'

'Why didn't you believe them?' I pounce.

'Because my staff and I had never seen any sign of rats. I run a tight ship.' He surveyed his spotless restaurant. 'And this is a competitive business; quite honestly, I thought someone was trying to sabotage me by spreading rumours. Then the Vaders appeared and found three dead rats in the kitchen, so clearly I was wrong.'

'But what if you weren't? What if the Vaders planted the dead rats there themselves and there were none to begin with?'

'Oh dear …' Monsieur Noiseau utters. I can

tell from his face that he's never considered this before.

'Can we have a look in your kitchen?' I ask.

'Of course.'

Monsieur Noiseau, still shaken, gets up and leads us into the restaurant kitchen. He doesn't notice me bringing my rucksack with me, but Julie does.

The kitchen reminds me of a high-tech lab with its long stainless-steel tables. Instead of test tubes, the shelves are filled with copper pots and pans, and plates. Sauce spoons dangle from shelves. I notice a small, dark area like a pantry bricked away at the far end. Inside is a selection of wine with plenty of room for one more. Julie raises her eyebrows at me and I adjust my rucksack, imagining the cool length of the chartreuse along my spine.

Alex points to a silver door. 'Is this the door that leads to the wine cellar?'

'Yes. Nobody can use that lift, unless accompanied by me or the sommelier.'

'What's a sommelier?' Alex asks.

'The wine waiter.'

'So why knock a hole through the wall underground?' Julie asks. 'The Vaders could have broken into the restaurant and got into the cellar through the lift.'

'We have an excellent security system. Motion detectors all around the restaurant. Facial recognition to activate the lift.' Monsieur Noiseau makes a point of opening the door to show us the 'mirror' inside. 'Knocking through the cellar wall was much smarter. There are cameras down there, but no alarms would go off. And they wouldn't be disturbed underground – well, until you came along.' He shakes his head and takes a flyer out of a drawer. It says 'RAT-O-KILL Pest Control' in big letters.

'The Vaders showed up just after the Michelin inspectors had threatened to take my stars away if I didn't fix the rat problem. I was in such panic that I didn't check their credentials. I hired them on the spot.' He slams the flyer on the table, still angry at himself.

'They were only here for one afternoon. I even showed them the wine cellar in case it was infested too. When I realised that they were using poison – which can be just as harmful to humans as rats – I switched to a different company who only used sonic repellents.'

'What's that?' I ask.

'A device that doesn't harm animals but makes them run away. It produces a high-pitched whir that humans can't hear,' he explains. 'Rats, on the other hand, can. Let me show you.' From the same drawer he takes out a black plastic box with a switch and presses it. A second later I feel like my brain is going to explode. The sound is unbearable, like a soprano singing a high F off-key while scratching her nails down a chalkboard.

'Stop it!' I yell, covering my ears. Monsieur Noiseau hurriedly switches it off and gives me a confused look.

'Only rats can hear that sound.'

'Only rats, autistic people and people with sensory disorders.' I wince.

'Hugo has sharp ears,' Alex explains. 'He's like Superman in that way. And others too.'

Alex's comment makes me smile. Pangea really is whole again.

'I'm sorry, Hugo. You're the first human I've met who can actually hear that sound.' Monsieur Noiseau puts the sonic repellent back in the drawer.

'Wait a minute …' Alex suddenly grabs the flyer from the table. 'I've seen this somewhere before.' He rummages through the pockets of his jacket and pulls out a crumpled piece of paper. It's warped and wavy with water damage, but it's the exact same flyer. Except that someone has scribbled something on the back. A list of wines, most still legible, all with double names: Romanée-Conti. Puligny-Montrachet. Gevrey-Chambertin. This must be the list Vader One was talking about. I'm guessing it's the same thing Vader Two sneaked a look at before evidently dropping it in the wine cellar. He really did have a memory like a sieve.

'I found it in the wine cellar while you and Julie were sleeping,' Alex explains, not meeting my eyes. 'I decided to write a letter to Mum after all.'

'Don't worry, we won't read it,' I tell him. Alex's cheeks are cherry red. 'Just show the list to Monsieur Noiseau.'

Noiseau takes the flyer after Alex has folded back the half with his own cramped and messy writing on. The colour drains from Noiseau's face as he reads the names, like someone has pulled a plug.

'Any clue as to who was behind the theft?' I ask.

'Uh, yes, there is. But I need to sit down first.' Somehow Bertrand appears yet again, guiding Noiseau to a chair. The chef's legs are wobbly like jelly.

'Would you like some cognac, Monsieur?' Bertrand keeps a comforting hand on Noiseau's shoulder.

'Yes, please.' Noiseau sighs and rubs his forehead. 'A large one.'

Bertrand disappears again.

Noiseau clears his throat. 'This is a list of the world's best and rarest bottles of Bourgogne wine,' he begins in a shaky voice. 'Bottles I acquired at a Sotheby's auction this spring, and that were stolen from my wine cellar, among others. Another chef, Bartoli, was bidding against me at that auction, and I beat him. Not long after, a magazine called *The Wine Observer* awarded the Gold Award to my restaurant for what they called "a passionate devotion to the quality of its Bourgogne wine selection". That's like the Oscars of the wine world. Every chef in Paris sent me their congratulations. Except for Bartoli. He was fuming. Shortly after the award, rumours began about a rat infestation in my restaurant. Bartoli publicly called me "Chef Ratatouille"! I hired a lawyer, but I could never prove that he was the one who started the rumours.'

'Maybe it's time for the police to pay a visit to Bartoli?' I suggest.

Before we leave, and while Monsieur Noiseau

is pacing the restaurant on the phone to the police, I discreetly put the chartreuse with the other bottles in the kitchen. I know it's the right thing as soon as I do it, my mind and my rucksack feeling instantly lighter.

Alex and Julie look back at me from the doorway where they're keeping watch. I flash them a thumbs up.

THE SCHOOL
NEWSPAPER ROOM

When we step outside the restaurant, I pat Alex on the back.

'Well done, Alex! That was the last piece of the puzzle.'

'Thanks. You think I'll get the flyer back?'

I only saw Alex's letter for a couple of seconds, but I know exactly what it said. I know that Alex loves his mum very much. And that he can be surprisingly poetic.

'Of course. As soon as the police are done with it, you'll get it back.'

Looking satisfied, Alex puts on a pair of

sunglasses. Ones with a red plastic frame and blue arms.

'Hey! We have the same sunglasses!'

'Do we?' Alex says. 'I hadn't noticed. My eyes have been super sensitive to light since we left the underground. My doctor said I should wear sunglasses until it goes way.'

'But ...' It's on the tip of my tongue to say that we only spent five hours underground; there's no way he developed a light sensitivity in that brief time. And even if he had, why would he choose to wear the exact same sunglasses as me? Unless ... unless he's copying me deliberately?

I notice Julie smirking and realise that I'm right. My face breaks into a smile.

'What?' Alex says.

'Nothing. The sunglasses look great on you,' I say.

'Thanks. Yours too.'

Zoé meets us at the bus stop as our designated chaperone. We hop on the 42. It's not the fastest route (we have to change at

Concorde), but it's the most beautiful one. It stops at the *Tour Eiffel* (the Eiffel Tower).

We sit at the back of the bus. All three of us together. Zoé sits a few seats in front. She said she'd rather be mistaken for a tourist than for one of us 'children'.

I'm not sure what to do with myself; how to look like I belong there. I settle for putting one foot on the back of the seat in front like I've seen other kids do. It's not very comfortable.

'It was because of the BeeRocs,' Alex says suddenly, as I put my foot back down again.

'What?'

'The trainers. The ones you have at home. The ones *everyone* has except me. My mum can't afford them. The day you wore them to school, I got so angry. I mean, you couldn't care less what you wear! And then Arthur came, and he said I could hang out with them even though I'm younger and don't have BeeRocs, but I had to tip the milk over your head. So I did. I'm sorry. It was stupid.'

So it happened just because of some trainers?

'What shoe size are you?' I ask.

'Huh? Thirty-eight. Why?'

'Same here. You can have my BeeRocs. I don't like laces. Velcro is much more efficient.'

Mum got the BeeRocs to encourage me to learn to tie my shoes. I think it was Mathilde's idea, but my brain is just not wired that way.

'Are you sure?' Alex asks, wide-eyed. 'They're super expensive.'

'In an age where mankind is about to colonise Mars, I really don't see the point in sticking to an outdated product design like shoelaces,' I say. 'I'm a Velcro guy.'

The following day, we meet in the IT classroom that doubles as the school newspaper room. The first thing Nina does is apologise for calling me a stalker in the canteen. I accept the apology, and the chair she pulls out next to her as we sit down at one of the tables.

You don't get interviewed by Nina unless

you've accomplished something major, something newsworthy. Like breaking the fifty-metre record in butterfly held since 1976. Or getting locked in a cellar, escaping the Green Devil, crawling over bones, meeting crazy cataphiles, running from the police, attending an underground book launch and solving a wine theft.

As we tell Nina about our journey, I still can't believe that all of it happened for real.

'Why did you go underground in the first place?' Nina asks me.

'I was looking for friends. And I hoped to find them underground.'

'Did you?'

'Yes, but not in the way I thought I would.'

'I think what Hugo wants to say is that we rediscovered our friendship underground,' Julie explains. 'The three of us.'

'And why did you two decide to follow Hugo underground?'

'It was all about the adventure for me,' Alex says. 'That's who I am. An explorer. A pioneer.

I'm always looking to break new boundaries.'
Of course, Julie and I know that this isn't quite
true, but we stay silent.

'If I had lived 500 years ago,' he adds, 'I'd
have been a Viking or something.'

'More like 957 years ago,' I correct. 'The
Viking Age ended in 1066.'

'Whatever. My point is, I'm a trailblazer.'

Nina tries to get us back on track. 'So that
guy Bartoli was really behind the robbery?' she
asks.

Julie nods. 'They found all the stolen wine at
Bartoli's restaurant.'

'He wouldn't have been able to sell it,' I add.
'It would have been much too obvious that it
was stolen. He just wanted to strip Noiseau of
his Gold Award and destroy his reputation.
Instead, he destroyed his own.'

I'm thinking of another recent article, this
one from *Le Monde* – a much bigger newspaper
than our school one. I loved the headline:
'Affaire Bartoli: Les carottes sont cuites!'
Meaning it's all over for Bartoli. His chips are

down. The writing is on the wall. His carrots *and* his goose are cooked. All because he was jealous of Noiseau's wine award, of his cooking competition, the Noiseau d'Or, and of his three Michelin stars. Bartoli only had two.

'Bartoli posted fake rat rumours and testimonials online,' I continue. 'Then he hired the Vaders to pose as employees of a pest control company. They left dead rats around *L'Accord* to support the infestation rumours and gain access to the wine cellar. Noiseau would never have let them down there without proof.'

'But why all that drilling and underground drama?' Nina asks. 'Why didn't they steal the wine from inside the restaurant?'

'That was the plan, but security up to and including the lift was too tight. Inside the cellar they only had to worry about the cameras – hence the masks. In the end the Vaders had no other choice than to break into the cellar via the underground.'

'And that's where you came in,' Nina says,

sounding awed as the story comes full circle. 'This sounds like the script for a heist film!'

'Only better,' Alex smirks.

'Is that enough for the article?' Julie asks as Nina closes her notebook and reaches for the school camera.

'More than enough! I just need a photo. You'll be celebrities when this comes out.'

'So are we cataphiles now?' Alex wonders after Nina has left, still lost in his visions of glory. 'Like, crime-fighting cataphile detectives?'

'I don't know. We don't even have cave names yet,' I point out.

'Why don't we pick names for each other now?' Julie suggests. The timing is perfect. Mum says you know people well once you've shared a hotel room. Well, I think you know people *really* well when you've survived the underground together.

'You should be Brain,' Alex says, pointing at me. 'You know a lot of stuff.'

'Or Theseus, after the Greek hero who went

inside the labyrinth to kill the Minotaur,' Julie says. 'Without you, we would've been lost in the underground maze.'

Theseus. I do love Greek mythology.

'What about Dolphin for you, Julie?' Alex suggests. Julie thinks for a moment, tilting her head.

'I like Medusa,' she says.

'The Greek goddess?' I ask, confused. 'She had snakes instead of hair. I don't think that's a good fit. You have beautiful hair.'

Julie laughs. 'No! Medusa is another name for jellyfish. They're the most energy-efficient swimmers.'

I absorb this new fact. Medusa is perfect for Julie. Next I consider Alex and what would suit him. He loves BeeRocs, lasagne and his mum, but none of those lend themselves to a cool cave name.

'What about Leif for Alex?' I suggest. After Leif Eriksson, the Viking explorer who discovered America?'

'Leif?' Alex echoes. 'Leif …' he repeats,

seemingly trying it on for size. 'Yeah, I like it! Thanks, Theseus.'

At last: a nickname I like. And one that gives me an idea ...

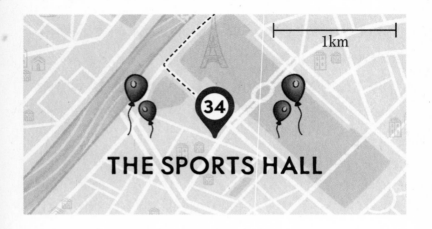

THE SPORTS HALL

There were many options that appealed to me: Sherlock Holmes. The Incredible Hulk. Superman. From a practical point of view, all three were possible. I could have borrowed Dad's trench coat for Sherlock Holmes. It has a cape, which would make me look very British. For the Hulk, I could have painted my face green and worn a pair of ripped jeans since I don't have any purple trousers (honestly, who does?). Or Mum said she could make a red cape really quickly if I wanted to be Superman.

But in the end, I decided that I didn't want to be any of them.

'Are you sure about this?' Zoé asks, eyeing

my legs, which are bare except for shin guards made from faux leather place mats. She'd been happy enough to cut up one of her old school skirts when I asked. It's a bit late to change her mind now it's shredded.

'I think you look great,' Dad says. Mum is prevented from saying anything by the needle in her mouth as she finishes tacking a silk scarf around the weighted vest. I haven't worn it since we got it back from the dry cleaners. Mum's scarf has transformed it from blue to bronze.

'There, try that,' she says, snipping the thread and plucking the needle from her lips.

A soothing feeling of calmness sets in as I put on the vest. I think of Temple Grandin's hug machine and the chatière in the underground. I fetch my sword and shield and look in the mirror; Theseus the Minotaur slayer looks back. Underneath the black slats of Zoé's ruined skirt, flashes of what was once a white ghost costume, newly shortened, show through. It gives the impression of a tunic beneath the armour.

By the time the doorbell rings, I've wrapped one of Dad's belts twice around my waist and added a red cape (I took Mum up on that offer). It's Alex and Julie at the door. Julie is dressed in a full-body swimming costume and holds a trident. Alex wears a horned Viking helmet and holds a hammer in his right hand.

'Love the costume!' Julie greets me. 'I'm Aquagirl. He's Thor.' She points at Alex.

'Can I try on your BeeRocs, Hugo?' Alex asks.

'Sure!' I take Alex and Julie to my room. Julie looks at the London tube map on my bedroom wall.

'It really does look like an abstract painting,' she says.

'I had no idea you remembered that,' I say, surprised. I hand the BeeRocs to Alex.

'I remember everything. Even that Doha in Qatar has one of the world's most advanced metro systems,' she smiles. I would love to show her my book *Transit Maps of the World*, but it will have to wait. The party is about to begin.

It turns out that Alex's feet are a little bigger than mine, even if we share the same shoe size. He doesn't care a bit.

'I can really have them?' he asks, as if he still can't believe his luck. 'For keeps?'

'Sure. I told you, I'm a Velcro guy,' I explain. Alex hugs me so tightly that I gasp for air.

'I just hope that my feet don't grow any more,' he says by my ear.

'You're still growing,' I remind him. 'So that seems unlikely.'

'Speaking of which,' he says, letting me go and rummaging in his pockets. 'I have something for you too.'

He hands me something small, metal and very familiar – although I haven't seen it since well before Alex and I stopped being friends.

'Your favourite toy car,' I say, turning the orange and blue striped concrete mixer in my hands. I hadn't expected this.

'Yours too. Remember when we were little, how you used to spin it until the colours melted into one, and you got all excited?'

I nod. There's something calming and comforting and beautiful about things that spin. Coasters, jar lids, spinning tops. And concrete mixer toy cars.

'I remember,' I say. 'I just didn't think *you* did.'

'Of course I do. You were my best friend.'

I nod again. My eyes sting.

'Go on then,' Alex says.

'What?' I croak.

'Spin it.'

So I do, and together we watch the colours merge.

The school sports hall is packed with kids in superhero costumes. The music is loud. Coloured disco lights circle around. They remind me of our torch beams slashing the darkness underground.

I am not sure how long I'll survive in this hostile environment of light and sound, but

I'm not worried. I brought my earplugs and sunglasses. I told Alex and Julie that I might have to leave early, or take breaks to reset my brain.

'Just tell us when it's getting too much for you, OK?' Julie reminds me. But so far, I feel OK.

I spot Enzo glowing in the corner. He's dressed as Iron Man, and I have to admit he looks great – surprisingly convincing with his LED Arc Reactor. I give him a thumbs up and he smiles at me. Then I notice one of Julie's teammates cutting a path towards us. He's dressed as Michelangelo – the Teenage Mutant Ninja Turtle, I mean. Not the sculptor.

'Cool costume,' Alex says.

'Thanks.' He stops in front of me. 'Hugo, is it true that there are giant piranhas in the underground? I heard you outswam five of them.'

'Ten,' Alex corrects him.

'No,' I say at the exact same time.

Nina's article isn't out until tomorrow, but

clearly rumours are already circulating about our underground adventure.

Julie chimes in. 'But there *was* a giant octopus.'

'*An octopus?*' Michelangelo's eyes are wide behind the orange bandana. He looks to me for confirmation, as if he knows that I can't lie.

I shrug, remembering Kaos's graffiti. 'It's true, there was a pretty big octopus.'

While the hero in a half shell digests this, Julie turns to Alex and me.

'Wanna dance?' she asks. Alex shakes his head. He never dances. Usually he just taps his foot whenever music comes on. But today he doesn't even do that. He's too busy looking down at the BeeRocs. He almost walked into a lamp post on our way here.

'What about you, Hugo?' Julie gives me a smile; the kind of smile that Mum or Mathilde gives me whenever they try to convince me of something I'm not super enthusiastic about.

'Just give me some time to adjust,' I say. I'm

already dealing with the noise and the roving lights. Adding another challenge involving gross motor skills like dancing might result in an operating system crash. Julie smiles and moves to the dance floor, circling her arms to the music.

'Hey, Alex! You came dressed as a handyman?' I immediately recognise Arthur. He's dressed as Batman.

'Alex is actually a Viking superhero from the Marvel Universe called Thor,' I explain. 'He's based on Norse mythology. Thor's weapon of choice is a hammer, but he isn't a handyman, he's a god.'

'Did I ask you something, weirdo?' Arthur snaps. 'Beat it.'

Then he turns back to Alex. 'So your mum finally got the BeeRocs? About time. Wanna hang out?'

'No, thanks,' Alex says pointing his hammer at me. 'I'm with Hugo.'

A warm feeling washes over me, and I wave even though I'm standing right next to him.

'Spy?' Arthur asks incredulously. 'Dude, he's wearing a skirt!'

'And you're wearing your pants outside your trousers.'

'No, I'm–' Arthur looks down in the middle of his denial, as if to confirm that he's not wearing black and grey spandex, but the newer, cooler Kevlar Batsuit – with underwear underneath, hopefully. Alex takes the opportunity to walk away with me.

'Hey handyman!' Arthur shouts after us. 'Don't bother trying to hang out with us again.'

'Deal!' Alex grins at me. 'Thor is part of the Marvel Universe anyway.'

I stop walking abruptly. 'Theseus isn't part of any cinematic universe. He's mythological.'

'Then I hereby dub you on honorary member of the MCU.' Alex flourishes his hammer like a sword and knights me on each shoulder.

'What about Julie? Aquagirl is DC like Batman.'

'OK, fine.' Alex rolls his eyes. 'Let's just agree to be friends whatever universe we're in. Deal?'

'Deal,' I say, and it's my turn to grin.

Julie returns as I'm advising Alex against throwing his empty plastic cup on the floor and demanding 'ANOTHER!' cola.

'Enough dancing,' she says, her face sweaty. It's warm in here, and loud, and bright.

'I think I need a break,' I say.

We leave the sports hall and sit down on the grass in front of the school. The place where Alex emptied the milk over my head. But so much has changed since then. From here, I can see the glass windows of the swimming pool where I was so unnecessarily rescued.

I turn to Alex and Julie. 'What are you doing tomorrow?'

When I come home from the superhero party, I find a letter on the kitchen table. It's addressed to me.

Dear Hugo,

First, I must scold you. You went underground when I told you not to. Hugo! But ... what can I say? You found a way in, which means that you must have been ready to go. And you won't believe what's happened since.

Philippe Noiseau came to the library. He showed me a letter that the police found in his cellar and only just returned to him: the letter you wrote to your family, of course.

We were both very impressed by your bravery, and Monsieur Noiseau wanted me to have the bottle of chartreuse as a token of his gratitude to you. He told me that without you and your friends, the best of his wine collection would have been lost.

You should be very proud of what you've done. Rest assured that I will spread the word about your underground adventure — and I hope to hear all about it next Tuesday.

Until then, from your friend
           and fellow cataphile,

                    Claudine

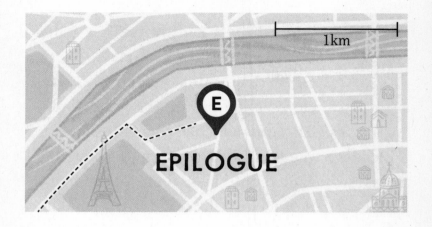

EPILOGUE

The swimming pool still smells of chlorine, but at least the fluorescent lights don't bother me. Zoé gave me some cool polarised goggles as an I'm-Glad-You-Didn't-Die-in-the-Underground-and-Don't-Ever-Do-That-to-Me-Again gift. Not far away, Julie is practising her backstroke, but Alex says that *I'm* the one who looks like an Olympic swimming champ.

I'm floating on my back. Water has entered my ears and the echoing voices of the other swimmers seem far away now, like the sounds of Paris underground. I close my eyes. I float for a few more minutes because it feels great to be weightless, the water filling my ears like liquid earbuds. Then I right myself as Julie swims back towards me.

'CANNONBALL!' Alex screams to our left, just before he jumps into the pool. Water splashes all around us. Then a whistle blows; a lifeguard wagging his finger from the edge. At least Alex waited until I was done floating.

Seeing me wince at the sound of the whistle, he swims up to us. 'Sorry. Wanna race?'

Julie snorts. 'Please! I need more of a challenge than that.'

'How about seeing who can hold their breath the longest?' I suggest.

'I can hold my breath for ten minutes!' Alex brags.

'Ten minutes?' Julie laughs. 'You wish!'

'The Bajau people can do it for even longer,' I say. 'They're sea nomads in Southeast Asia who live almost entirely on seafood. They can stay underwater for thirteen minutes while hunting. Their bodies have genetically adapted to be better at diving.'

'Like the insects and fish adapted to life in

the underground lab?' Alex asks.

'Exactly.'

'Well, the world record is nearly twenty-five minutes,' Julie says. 'Want to give it a go?'

Without another word, all three of us duck underwater. The last time I was down here, all I could see were people's legs, their top halves distorted above the surface of the water. Now Alex and Julie are down with me.

Alex's underwater face reminds me of a pufferfish. Julie bounces on the pool's floor, cross-legged with her eyes closed like she's meditating, waving her arms to stay down there. After just thirty seconds, Alex darts out of the water. Five seconds later, Julie does too.

I'm the last to emerge.

'Fifty seconds!' Julie smiles. 'Nice.'

'No world record, though,' Alex points out, high-fiving me all the same.

'Or going to live with the Bajau,' I agree.

We climb out of the pool and sit on a plastic bench near the edge. I keep my heels lifted so that only my big toes touch the floor. I still don't like the idea of all those smelly, sweaty, wart-infested feet.

'What are you doing after school on Tuesday?' Julie asks. 'I don't have swimming practice.'

'On Tuesdays I go to the library,' I reply. '2 to 4 p.m.'

'Cool. Can I go with you? I'd love to see the old underground maps you told me about.'

'Me too,' Alex says. 'Who knows what other adventures they might come in useful for …'

'Oh no!' Julie shakes her head vigorously. 'Never again. This,' she stresses, jerking her chin towards the pool, 'is my element. Right here. Down there I'm way out of my depth.'

'That's why we've got Hugo,' Alex insists. 'The underground is *his* element.'

'No,' I disagree. 'It isn't.'

'Really? Then where is?'

Not 'where', I want to say, but *who*. It doesn't matter where I am, but who is there with me.

I look to either side of me; at Julie on my left and Alex on my right. Then I look out across the pool, to where three abandoned swimming floats have drifted together: a multicoloured island in an ocean of blue.

I smile.

Where's my element? The place I belong?

'Like Julie said: it's right here.'

ACKNOWLEDGEMENTS

It takes a village to make a book ...

Thank you to my stellar agent Silvia Molteni at Peters, Fraser + Dunlop in London, who took the risk on an unknown writer from Luxembourg with a manuscript set in the Paris underground. *Mille grazie*, Silvia, for believing in me.

Thank you to the entire team at Sweet Cherry Publishing, and especially to my brilliant editor Kellie Jones. Thank you for helping me shape the story and bring it to life. You are my literary midwife.

Thank you to all the wonderful people who have worked with me on this story over the years before it became BOY UNDERGROUND. Tricia Rayburn and Maryrose Wood, thank you for your insights into story structure.

I am grateful to Gilles Thomas for having written *Atlas du Paris souterrain* and many more books on the Paris underground. I relied on Robert Macfarlane's brilliant book *Underland: A Deep Time Journey* for the description of the underground maps. Thank you also to Lazar Kunstmann, author of *La culture en clandestins. L'UX* and founding member of the UX.

Thank you to my fabulous high school English teacher, Germain Dondelinger (1953–2015). You're part of the reason I write in English today.

A special thank you to my family and especially to my son Eli who inspired this story with his map obsession. Eli never went underground, but like Hugo he has a photographic memory, and he will always be able to tell you the best Métro connection between *Châtelet* and any other point in Paris. He's also a Velcro guy, by the way.

And finally, thank you to my wonderful parents who many years ago gave me a red typewriter that started it all. Mum, I wish you were still around to read my book.

Clock Tower Publishing was launched in 2021 and is a trade imprint of Sweet Cherry Publishing. We champion new, marginalised and diverse voices in publishing, inspired by our multicultural Leicester heritage. We aim to bring our readers a range of high-quality fiction that authentically showcases the diverse and inclusive world we live in while hooking them in a compellingly great story. From fantasy fiction to future classics, we're dedicated to creating a great list of quality trade fiction that's championed by its authors and illustrators alongside a diverse team of book lovers.

www.clocktowerpublishing.com